GRAVE CONSEQUENCES

PENNSYLVANIA PARKS SERIES

by Elle E. Kay

Many blessings!

Elle E. Kay

Grave Consequences

PENNSYLVANIA PARKS

Faith Writes Publishing

PO BOX 494

BENTON PA 17814-0494

Ebook ISBN: 978-1-950240-37-1

Paperback ISBN: 978-1-950240-40-1
Hardback ISBN: 978-1-950240-41-8

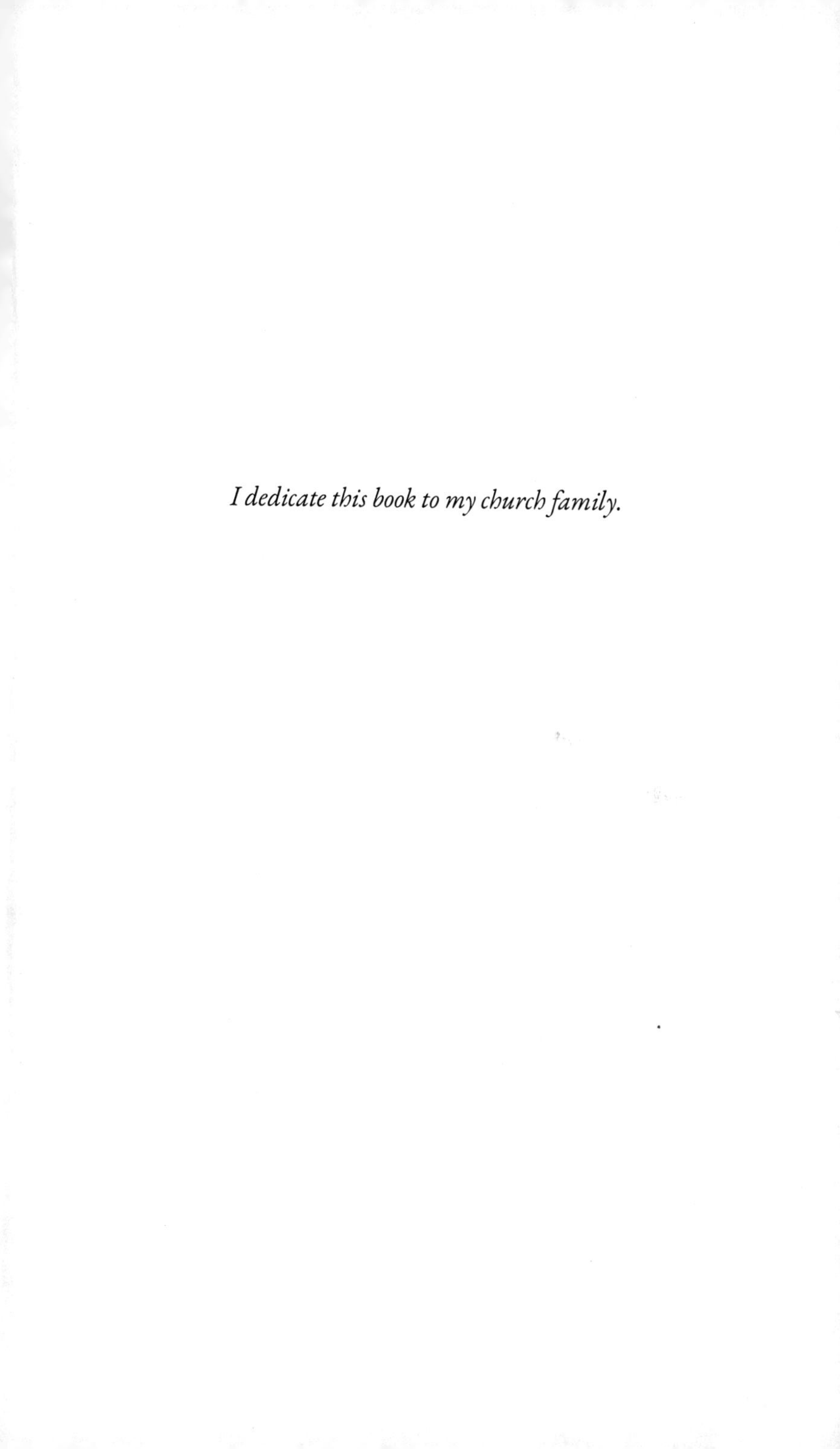

I dedicate this book to my church family.

"The Lord is not slack concerning his promise, as some men count slackness; but is longsuffering to us-ward, not willing that any should perish, but that all should come to repentance."

—2 Peter 3:9 (KJV)

[Emphasis added.]

Chapter One

Malachi sipped his lukewarm coffee and watched a group pull into the lot in a 1970's lime-green Volkswagen bus. He'd seen a few in car shows, but this was the first brightly colored one he'd spotted in the wild since his boyhood. In anticipation of a check-in, he headed to the front desk. There was a familiarity to them, so he searched his memories for a reason, but came up blank. They may have camped there before. That would explain it. One guy entered the office while his friends stayed outside. "Camping reservations?"

"Yeppers." A slow smile crept across his face as he handed him a cell phone with reservation information displayed on the screen. Name on the booking was Reece Mclean.

"Seven days?" Malachi studied the man's face. There was nothing remarkable about his features, but he had a quiet presence about him that seemed at odds with the crowd outside.

Something nagged at the edges of his consciousness. Why did he feel like he should know who this man was?

"That's the plan." The slow cadence of the stranger's lazy speech brought back a time he'd rather forget. Evenings spent with the other children chasing fireflies. A childhood that should've been magical, but became a nightmare.

He shook away his past and forced his focus back to the man. "You from West Virginia?" Malachi took a long draw from his coffee and waited for an answer.

"I stayed there a while." The man smiled. "You been there?"

"A lifetime ago."

Malachi handed him the keys to cabin seven and circled the location on a map. "You're all set. Enjoy your stay." The guy studied him a moment before turning to leave.

He shrugged off his uneasiness and watched through the window until the group's van pulled out of the lot.

Frost crunched beneath his boots as Malachi followed the blood trail through the woods. Poachers likely snagged a deer. He crossed Loyalsock Creek and picked the trail up again on the other side. If he found the gut pile, it would confirm his suspicions. A blatant disregard for game regulations, but there was little to be done. Park rangers and game wardens handed out citations. But more than half the time, the offenders didn't pay their tickets nor did they bother to buy a hunting license in the first place, so restricting them was less than useless.

The sun glinted off an empty chip bag, and he shook his head as he bent to retrieve it. When he stood, he noticed a patch of black fur caught on the bark of a hemlock tree. Could be from a bear. Or even a dog. Hard to tell from the tiny clump. His brow furrowed as he inspected the ground for drag marks and found more blood. He took in the surrounding area hoping to discover where the injured animal had been taken when he spotted the rocky outcropping. A bear den.

Without even looking, he knew he wouldn't find the bear inside. It'd been shot right inside the den. Closing his eyes for a moment, he braced himself for what came next. Hopefully, the bear who'd been shot and dragged from this den hadn't been a pregnant sow. Malachi peered into the opening. Empty. Stuffing his hands in his pockets to keep them warm, he took a deep breath of pine-scented air.

After an uneventful hike back to his truck, Malachi tapped his fingers on the wheel as he started up the engine. Why would anyone purposely harm the wildlife roaming these hills? Encountering a bear in the wilderness was a dream that remained unfulfilled for most people. Working at Worlds End State Park, he'd had his share of bear encounters, but for folks who worked nine-to-five jobs in the city and came out here once or twice in their lifetimes ... for them, those encounters were nothing short of miraculous. And someone had taken the life of one of their bears. He huffed out a breath, more than ready to unravel the thin threads he'd found and identify the person responsible for the loss. When he arrived back at the office, he hurried inside, hung his jacket on the back of his chair, and logged into some hunting forums, hoping the poacher had been stupid enough to post a trophy photo. No such luck. Not a bear to be found. He discovered posts about trophy bucks that might be worth looking into, but they often didn't amount to anything more than fish tales accompanied by stolen pictures. He'd take a look at the EXIF data to determine whether any were legitimate and worth taking the time to investigate.

A burst of cold air hit him as the door swung open and a young woman with ginger hair braided in pigtails walked in. Judging by her khakis and the green jacket with a Game Commission patch on it, she wasn't a park visitor.

"Can I help you?" He stood to greet her.

"I hope so. I'm Cate Garrison, biologist with the Game Commission." She held out her hand, and he shook it. "We have a radio-collared bear in the area that we planned to check in on next week, but we lost her signal yesterday morning. I'd like to check and make sure she's still in her den before the rest of the team joins me."

The Game Commission had moved faster than usual. He chuckled. "I'm Malachi James. A DCNR ranger here at the park, and I may know what happened to your bear. I'll take you to the den site, but it'll have to wait until morning. We're losing daylight fast."

She raised an eyebrow, and he noticed flecks of gold in her olive-green eyes. He pulled his focus away from her eyes and shoved his hands in his pockets.

"Followed a blood trail this morning that led me to the den. Looks like someone shot your sow and dragged her from the woods." He frowned. "The poacher who shot her likely destroyed the collar."

Her hands shook as she shoved them in her jacket pockets. "That isn't good. Not good at all."

"Everything all right?"

"She's the third bear poached from her den this year. And that's just the ones we're aware of."

"How many bears are you tracking?"

"A hundred or so across the state. One was taken from Promised Land. The other happened at Ricketts Glen." He thought her voice had a slight tremble and her chin dipped as she spoke, but then he thought he must've imagined it as she continued. "It's important that we get back to that den. This sow was among the first to hunker down this year, so we're relatively certain that she has cubs."

"I didn't see any." No way he would've missed them.

CATE HOPPED INTO HER Ford Ranger and banged her forehead on the steering wheel. *Ouch.* She tilted her head back and rubbed her forehead. How could it be too late to hike into the woods? Half past three. Tapping her short nails on the console, she considered her options. She could go alone. The voice of Virginia Vaughn echoed deep within her. *You can't protect the wildlife if you don't protect yourself.* Heading into the forest alone without a clear understanding of the den's proximity to the road might not be the most advisable approach for self-preservation. She blew out a breath. Fine. She'd wait until morning.

Gavin and Samantha wouldn't mind the company. Worlds End State Park wasn't far from the town of Benton and Ricketts Glen State Park where her brother's wife worked as a DCNR ranger. Sam might have some insight into how to go about finding the bear cubs. The buzzing of an incoming call pulled her from her thoughts. A picture of Gavin in uniform lit up her screen. She grinned. "What do you want?"

"Do you always answer the phone like that?"

"Only if it's you or Grayson."

"Nice. Glad to hear you reserve your rude behavior for your brothers." Sarcasm laced his voice. "Just calling to check in. How's work?"

"Challenging. You at home?"

"Yeah. Why?"

"I'm at Worlds End. Not too far from you, so I thought I might stop over."

"I've been there. It's about forty-five minutes from here and in the opposite direction of State College."

She bit her lip. He would make her ask. She should just get a room somewhere. It'd be easier. She breathed out a sigh. "I have to be back here tomorrow, so I thought..."

"You're more than welcome to stay at our place. But what about your cat?"

The corners of her lips lifted as she thought about her calico. "My landlady will take Penny until I get home. We have an arrangement."

"In that case, dinner should be ready when you get here."

"See you shortly."

She wasn't as far away as Gavin seemed to think. She'd make it there in thirty-five minutes. Not nearly enough time to prepare herself for the interrogation her older brother would put her through though. Dating anyone? Meet any friends? Have you thought any more about moving out this way? She could hear the rapid-fire questions before they even started. Maybe she should fish some ibuprofen out of her purse. If she'd been smart, she would've driven the two hours home and come back tomorrow rather than subjecting herself to Gavin. She smiled despite herself. Admitting she missed him was a bridge too far. Her brothers were over-protective and controlling, but they loved her fiercely and would do anything to keep her safe and happy.

Chapter Two

Cate pulled into her brother's driveway. He'd moved into the home where Samantha had grown up, but they'd made more than a few upgrades, doubling the size of the original house and completely customizing the interior. From the outside, it still looked like a nineteenth-century farmhouse.

Her sister-in-law pulled her in for a hug.

A delicious savory aroma filled the air with the scent of rosemary and something else? "I'm starved. What is that I'm smelling?"

"Chlorine."

"Not that, but come to think of it, why do I smell chlorine?" Cate asked.

"Ask your brother." Sam chuckled. "The aroma of food is from a pot roast."

Cate glanced around. "Where's my niece?"

"Aha!" Sam grinned. "I knew you didn't come to see us."

"Trina's with Grayson and Jenna. They took her to Disney World," Gavin said.

Cate bit back her disappointment at having missed seeing her niece and forced herself to smile. "Isn't three a little young for that?" Their father had sent them there a few times, but only managed to join them once. Age eight at the time, she barely remembered the visit.

He laughed. "You try telling them that."

She flopped down on their new sofa. "Ivory? Really? You'll be having it cleaned once a month."

"I told him the same thing." Sam made a tsk noise with her tongue.

He shook his head. "It was evident to me that you wanted this color and fabric because you kept going back to it."

"Totally impractical." Samantha sighed, but her eyes ignited in a way that Cate could tell Gavin had guessed correctly. Sam loved it. A buzzer went off. "Sounds like the garlic biscuits are ready. How about some food?"

"Yum." Cate followed her into the large open kitchen. "Wow, this place looks amazing."

Samantha glanced around the space. "I wish my parents could've seen it with all the upgrades we've made."

"I'm sure they would've loved it."

"Yes, but the solarium and indoor pool are excessive. I have no idea what Gavin was thinking."

"That explains the odor of chlorine." Cate took a seat at the farmhouse-style table made of solid oak. "I want to see it, but not until after I devour this comfort food you prepared."

"At least someone appreciates my cooking."

Gavin sank into the seat beside Cate. "I love your cooking.

Just wish you'd leave out the mushrooms. So many mushrooms."

Sam shrugged. "I like them."

He always did hate the fungus, but his teasing held no malice. "Ignore him."

MALACHI STOOD BY THE pellet stove and reveled in the warmth as he watched Titan, a one-hundred-pound Bernese Mountain dog, roll around on his back on the snow-covered lawn while Pixie, a five-pound cat, swatted at his face. Pixie jumped and spun in the air catching a snowflake on her nose. The dog gently nudged his snout against his little friend and the two of them ran to the door ready to be let in.

An icy breeze swept through the house as he let his pets in, so he quickly shut the door to keep the heat from escaping. He filled their bowls with kibble then watched as they stuck their noses into their food. Always happy to be fed. Never complaining.

Staring into the refrigerator, he tried to decide what to make for himself. He'd thawed out beef but didn't feel like making anything with it. Cooking for one felt like a waste of energy tonight. But he should be used to the life of a bachelor by now. There were few women who were able to tolerate a brooding, contemplative man. They wanted fun and games. An image of the ginger-haired girl who'd come into the office earlier flashed in his mind, but he pushed it away. She was a colleague. They would work together on this case. Nothing more.

The offerings found in his freezer didn't look all that promising, either. There were always Hot Pockets. Easy prep. No dirty dishes. After topping off his water, he shoved the quick meal into the microwave. It would suffice.

As the aroma of pepperoni and melted cheese filled the room, his mouth watered, and his stomach growled, a reminder that he hadn't eaten since breakfast. His laptop made lousy dinner company, but he hoped to find a lead worth following. The bear poacher wouldn't get away with it. Not too far in the past, a night hunter with a tendency to leave his kills to decay in the field was caught. He got off with a mere fine.

One at a time he checked groups and pages. Facebook. Instagram. TikTok. Twitter. Oh, right, X now. He pushed aside what little remained of his food and focused on his screen. Page after page of blathering posts filled with all the latest fish stories. But none of the usual haunts produced a lead worth following.

Malachi rose and tossed his paper plate in the trash, then carried his laptop into the living room. Once settled in his recliner, he opened the Nextdoor site. Not as popular as other social media. Posts were few and far between, but a number of locals used it and sometimes he'd find a nugget that proved helpful. He scrolled down the page. A post about a missing dog. Not one he'd seen, but he lifted a prayer that the pup would be found safe and sound. Another complaining about trespassers—that had potential. Possibly. Lastly, someone looking for suggestions for a local plumber.

Unfortunately, tonight hadn't been all that fruitful, but he'd follow up on the trespassers. It was possible that there might be something there. But, then again, it might be nothing. Sighing, he set down the laptop and rubbed his forehead. Tomorrow was another day. He'd take the biologist out to the den site and maybe they'd find some new piece of evidence that would produce a lead. Doubtful, but possible.

He flipped on the television and prepared to binge-watch *Person of Interest* on Prime. He wouldn't have any objections to having that kind of surveillance when he was working a case, but he was unwilling to sacrifice his privacy to acquire it. Titan brought him a ball while Pixie stared unblinkingly at them from her perch on the back of the couch. Malachi tossed it for him then laughed as the dog amused himself by bouncing it around and skittering after it.

In the rustic log cabin they'd rented, Reece stood in the doorway of one of the two bedrooms and watched Dorcas sleeping beside the twins, Benjamin and Bethany. The perfect portrait of innocence. If only his hands were as clean as his young wife's.

She exuded an understated beauty—some might even label her as plain—but she had a rosy way of looking at life that both annoyed him and intrigued him. He couldn't get her out of his system.

It was past time for him to move on. If he didn't, the law would catch up with him. Time was not in their favor, and he had doubts about her willingness to join him if he explained the need for a new chapter. Nevertheless, they had this moment. He moved the little ones onto the sleeping bags they'd brought and climbed into bed with his wife. Tonight, he'd lie beside her and watch her sleep. That would be enough.

Hours later he awakened to a scratching noise. At first, he chalked it up to tree branches rubbing against each other and scraping the roof of the cabin, but then he remembered what he'd done. Taking the life of the sow was one thing, but he hadn't found the strength to end the lives of her youngins. He'd enlist Becky's help taking care of them until he came up with a long-term solution. Some fish had figuratively nibbled at the hook he'd been floating, but none had taken a bite yet. It probably wouldn't be long before someone did and he'd have a buyer for the cubs. If not, he'd do what needed to be done and dispose of them, however distasteful.

Chapter Three

Cate tried to keep pace with Malachi as he scurried up the side of the mountain. There was no marked trail to take, but his sense of direction seemed flawless. She stopped to catch her breath, and before long, he turned back to check on her.

"You okay?"

"Fine, but I need a minute."

"Shouldn't you be used to hiking?" He made his way back to where she stood, leaning against the trunk of a Quaking Aspen.

She fought for breath to answer him. "I am."

The corners of his lips turned up a tad. "I promise it's not too much farther."

"I need a minute. Asthma."

"Sorry. Didn't realize." His eyes widened. "Do you have your inhaler?"

"It's in my backpack." She nodded. "I saw no reason to mention the affliction. Until now."

He helped her take the pack off her back and then rifled through it until he found her inhaler. "Here you go."

"Thanks." She placed the plastic between her lips and took a puff. Her chest expanded as it filled with air, and she held her breath. As she released it, the tightness in her chest loosened.

"I'm in these hills every day. I forget that not everyone is used to the terrain." Malachi scraped a hand across his neatly trimmed beard.

"I'm guessing you don't lead many group hikes."

"Not if I can help it."

"Grumpy introvert?"

His eyes shone with laughter. "Lone wolf."

"Same thing."

"The few groups I've led didn't appreciate my sense of humor."

She tilted her head and smiled. "I find that hard to believe." Not true. She absolutely believed it and wished she could've been on the hikes to see it for herself. In the short amount of time she'd known him, she already sensed he had a similar personality to her older brothers.

It had probably been about a minute. Time for a second inhale. She breathed in the medicine and held the breath before slowly releasing it. "I think I'm okay to keep going, but if you would slow your pace a tad, my lungs will thank you."

"Sure thing." He studied her a few seconds longer. "You sure you're okay to keep going?"

"I am."

"The trail is wide enough here that we can walk side by side."

True to his word, five minutes later they arrived. The pecking noise from a pileated woodpecker filled the air, and she searched for it among the barren forest. A tree stood nearby, lifeless and stripped of branches, but the bird found enjoyment in it. The song of a chickadee contrasted with the relentless banging, and she smiled as it tilted its head at them curiously.

They cautiously approached a rocky ledge, and she stared into a dark cleft in the rock. The strong odor of bear remained, but the air around it was cool. If the mother bear occupied the space, warmth would've emitted from it. Any cubs she'd had wouldn't have survived being left alone without their mother's body heat.

Cate went into a coughing fit. It would be another hour before she should use her inhaler again, so she waited for the coughs to subside on their own. When they did, she pointed her Maglite into the narrow cavern then scooted inside to inspect the den.

"You sure that's a good idea, Ms. Garrison?"

"It's Cate. And, yes, it's my job, Mr. James." She handed him her flashlight. "Hold this for me. I need to inspect the area."

After taking several photographs, Cate scooted back out through the small opening and showed Malachi the photographs she'd taken with her digital camera. "The amount of fur left behind along with the nesting material suggests she gave birth. And see these indentations?" She indicated the shallow dents in the nesting material.

He nodded.

"They're from her cubs. The evidence suggests there were three of them."

"What kind of monster kills a sow while she's in a den with her cubs? Do you think he killed the cubs?" A strain in his voice revealed his deep concern for the wildlife that inhabited the park where he worked. It had bothered her when he declined to hike out here with her the afternoon before, but now that she knew the distance to the site, she acknowledged to herself he had made the right decision. However, this wasn't the moment to contemplate Malachi and whether or not she concurred with his decisions. Right now, she needed to keep her focus on their conversation.

"It is impossible to determine what transpired with them. Another predator may have happened upon the den and taken them."

He frowned. "That part is my job. I'll find the guy who did this on park land, then find out from him if he left the cubs here or took them with him." He cracked his knuckles. "And I'll see that he's prosecuted for it."

"Or she."

"Doubtful."

"But possible."

"Admittedly, yes."

"I hope you catch whoever did this." She took some more photos of the area surrounding the den and marked the waypoint so she'd be able to find the location again.

Malachi waited for Cate to precede him on the trail to allow her to set the pace. He didn't want a repeat performance of the asthma attack she'd suffered on the way up the mountain. Working at the park he'd seen them before. Sometimes they manifested as wheezing. Other times, coughing fits. Most of the time, it had been children and the elderly who experienced them, often triggered by someone burning plastic at a nearby campsite. Occasionally he'd seen exertion or cold air bring them on. He didn't know much about the condition, but he hadn't expected to see a strong, capable woman suffer the effects. For some reason, seeing Cate in a vulnerable state made him want to protect her. And the last thing he needed was to form any attachments.

Their relationship was a professional one, but he couldn't help but notice how her fiery hair refused to stay neatly threaded inside her braids. And even though she wore a bulky Carhartt jacket, she was petite and physically fit beneath it from what he could tell.

She stopped short on the trail, and he almost ran into her. Turning to face him, she placed a finger to her lips and pointed at something in the distance. A buck rubbed his antlers on a sumac. Side by side, they watched the majestic being until it walked off in the opposite direction. "Amazing what you get to see in the woods when you slow down and take note of your surroundings."

He chuckled, recognizing the dig at his hurried pace on their way in. "When do you head back to your home base?"

"Trying to get rid of me, Ranger Rick?"

"It's Malachi, as you are fully aware."

"You need a nickname."

"Then come up with something more original."

"I'll do that." She tapped her forefinger to her chin. "How about Loyalsock Loner?"

He lifted an eyebrow. "You can do better than that."

"I'll work on it."

"If you're going to be here for some time, we could get something to eat." He shrugged.

"You mean like a date?" Her eyes widened.

"Just a bite to eat with a colleague."

"In that case, I'm in." She frowned. "I'm staying at my brother's house while I'm in the area. He's quite a distance from here. Would you mind an early dinner, so I don't have to drive all the way back?"

"There aren't too many places around here, so we could meet closer to your brother's house if that works for you."

After a beat of silence, she responded. "I don't want to inconvenience you."

"Where does he live?" he asked.

"Benton."

It wasn't nearby, but he regularly drove that distance since nothing was in close proximity. "Let's eat there this time, and next time we'll pick somewhere in the middle."

The corner of her mouth twisted in something resembling a smile. "What makes you think there will be a next time?"

"Just a feeling I get." He winked and continued down the trail. When they reached the park office, he handed her his personal cell phone. "Put your number in it, and I'll call you when I'm on my way to Benton."

Chapter Four

Becky adjusted her long woolen skirt as she settled onto the park bench. A park ranger walked some redhead to her car. It might be him, but she couldn't confirm from the distance.

Coming north had been her suggestion. She hoped to find him, but she'd never expected Reece to agree with her scheme. Plans were being formulated, and she needed to be ready for the worst. She'd outlived her usefulness to the community. The peaceful setting reminded her of her childhood in the Appalachians. Becky stood and stretched. It wasn't far back to the cabin, but she'd take her time returning there. A white-tailed deer meandered at the edge of the creek. A flash of red caught her eye, and she followed it to a nearby tree where a pair of cardinals landed. If only she possessed the same freedom to flit about. Despite the winter chill hovering just below freezing, these mountains bustled with wildlife.

A man with a backpack slung over his shoulder and a walking stick in his right hand exited a nearby trail onto the dirt road. Something about him reminded her of Benjamin. She shut her eyes against the memories of Ben lying in a shallow grave, his eyes wide open in horror as shovelfuls of dirt covered him. If Reece had known she lurked in the shadows, watching, he might've shot her, too. It was impossible to be sure, and she didn't plan to tell him what she'd observed. Better to stay invisible. Under the radar.

The man gave a nod, acknowledging her presence, and she smiled in greeting. Her smile was fake. Plastic. It described her well. A sigh escaped as she approached the bend leading back to the cabin.

Dorcas stood at the fire ring stirring a pot of chili over the campfire. The wretch hummed to herself. Always pleasant. Never fake. Delusional. A true believer. In her eyes, Reece could do no wrong. Once upon a time, Becky felt the same way about Ezekiel. Truth be told, she still did.

Becky's lip curled as she stared at the younger woman. Once upon a time, she'd been just like her. Life had a way of stealing a person's idealism.

Cate's eyes widened, and she stared at her brother who stood in front of the huge fireplace in his living room.

"What?" His forehead crinkled as he narrowed his gaze. "We don't even know this guy."

"He's a colleague, Gavin." She rolled her eyes heavenward. "You may have forgotten, but I am an adult, and I can have dinner with anyone I want."

"Sam and I can join you. Vet the guy."

Sam placed a hand on her husband's arm. "Your sister is going on a date, Gavin. She doesn't want us tagging along."

"It's not a date."

"Then it's settled. We'll join you."

"No. We won't." Sam laughed. "You should hear yourself. How would you have felt if I had a big brother who had wanted to check you out?"

"It's not the same."

"Isn't it?"

"She's a target. Anyone who knows who our father is will want to get into her good graces." As many times as she'd heard this lecture, she might as well be living in the movie *Groundhog Day*, reliving the same conversation again and again.

Tapping her fingers on the edge of the sofa, she looked up at Gavin again. "Malachi is completely unaware of anything related to our father."

"How can you possibly know that?"

"Trust me. Besides, like I said, this is not a date. We'll probably talk about missing bear cubs through the entire meal."

"Missing cubs?" Gavin's eyebrows shot up.

"Yeah." Cate drew out the word.

"One of our tech guys mentioned someone trying to sell black bear cubs on the dark web."

"What was he doing on the dark web?"

"I didn't ask. I'm sure it had to do with one of our cases. He was in a forum for buying and selling exotic species."

Sam's brow crinkled. "Nothing exotic about bears."

That could be the reason it caught his attention and seemed strange to him.

Cate made eye contact with Samantha. "Did my goofy brother mention anything about this to you before now?"

"Not a word." Sam slowly shook her head.

"You didn't say anything sooner because?"

"Didn't correlate it with either of you. It was a random conversation with one of my employees. And I doubt it has anything to do with your missing cubs."

"Are you aware of whether the individual selling them is in Pennsylvania?" Sam asked.

"He didn't say."

Cate sighed. "Do you think it's possible for you to get your guy to find out more? If the cubs are here, the game cops could set up an undercover buy and get the cubs back and the perpetrators arrested."

"I'll see what I can find out."

"In the meantime, I better get going if I'm going to meet Malachi in time."

"Be careful driving," Sam said.

Gavin walked her to the door. "If you run into any trouble with this guy, text me. I'll be there forthwith."

"Relax. He's a nice guy."

His nod was barely perceptible.

ON MAIN STREET, BUSINESSES and homes abounded, most residing within the confines of historic Victorian houses. Dueling gas stations stood on the corner near the dam. Antique stores, a quaint coffee shop, and a couple of restaurants lined the road.

When Malachi arrived at The Filling Station, he pulled into the alley and parked around back. Inside, a warm glow from the overhead lighting welcomed him as a hostess guided him to a table near a window. A server soon appeared.

"Can I get you something to drink?"

"I'm waiting on someone, but yes, if you would bring two waters, that'd be great."

"Lemon?"

He didn't know if Cate wanted lemon or not, but she didn't have to use it. "Sure. Thanks." Soon, she appeared in the doorway and he waved her over. "I got you water to start, but you can ask for something else if you'd rather."

"Water's perfect. Thanks." She smiled. "Sorry I'm late. My brother had some interesting news."

"Yeah?"

"He claims someone is trying to sell black bear cubs."

"Where at?"

"I'm not very familiar with all the details, but he mentioned that one of his tech guys stumbled upon the post on an exotic animal sales forum on the dark web where someone was trying to sell black bear cubs."

"Around here?"

"He's going to see if he can find out where the post originated."

"Even if it isn't the cubs from the den we inspected, it's a travesty."

"Most of what happens on those forums is. Or so I've been told."

"You don't peruse the dark web in your free time?" He glanced out the window at the peaceful small town certain that like the dark web, it held its own secrets, but not sure he wanted to uncover them.

Her green eyes lit up when she laughed. "I haven't yet developed that hobby."

The server returned and took their orders. They each ordered a burger and fries.

"So, any other suggestions on how to find the cubs if the dark-web thing doesn't pan out?"

"I've been scouring social media hoping for a glimpse of them, but nothing yet."

"They might've been left in the den." She frowned. "There is a chance that a predator took them."

"You didn't see any signs that they'd been killed there, right?"

"No. It didn't look like a coyote or another predator had been in there. If I had to guess, I would say the poacher took them." She pushed one of her braids back behind her shoulder. "That doesn't mean they're alive though. He might've killed them."

"True." He scratched his chin. "But I'm hopeful that he didn't."

"Optimistic. I like it." She grinned. "Opposite my brothers."

"You have brothers? Tell me about them."

"Pessimistic. Obviously." She squeezed the lemon into her water and wiped the sweat off her glass with a napkin, then took a long sip. "Protective. Big-hearted."

"I've been properly warned. Beware protective elder brothers."

"That's good advice. They own a private security company." She took another sip of water and set her glass down. "My brothers wreak havoc on my dating life."

"I'll bet bodyguard big brothers are a sufficient deterrent for most men."

"Yes. They sure are." A troubled look briefly crossed her features, and he wondered if he'd imagined it. She twirled one of her braids around her index finger. "It's aggravating."

"I would think it must be nice to have someone who cares about you enough to intimidate anyone who might be less than genuine."

"I guess so." She released her braid as the server set their burgers down. "That came out quickly. And it smells divine."

It did indeed. "I'm starved." Not just for food. For company. And hers was what he needed tonight, a pleasant combination of serious and sassy. He could get used to spending time with her.

Chapter Five

Dust danced in the sunbeams streaming in the enormous windows lining the spare room Cate currently occupied at her brother's house. The moment had arrived to provide her boss with an update. Virginia Vaughn hated email and text. She preferred phone calls. Telephones were Cate's nemesis. She needed to make calls for work, but experienced a touch of panic before each one. It wasn't a mere dislike of using them. It was a fear. And every once in a while, it was debilitating enough that no amount of self-talk could make her dial it.

The same thing didn't happen when she called her brothers, and receiving calls was slightly less traumatizing, but dialing the telephone could be paralyzing. Her fears might be irrational. She could accept that, but it didn't make them go away. She did as much as possible through email or text, but on those rare occasions when she couldn't, she needed to spend fifteen minutes psyching herself up.

She punched in the number and waited out the rings, forcing herself to remain on the line.

“Hello.”

“I have an update for you.” Cate shared what they’d found so far. “I’m hoping for some time to investigate the disappearance of the cubs.”

“That’s why we have Game Commission officers and DCNR rangers. It’s not your job to find them, Cate.”

“I know, but I think I can help. If the cubs are found, law-enforcement won’t be able to tend to them until they can be placed.”

“We don’t have much time left, Cate. Hibernation doesn’t last forever. We have to do our work now.”

“Please let me see this through.”

“You were aware when you accepted this position that there would be heartbreak, hon. This isn’t like books and movies where you get a happy ending every time. Saving the cubs may not be possible.”

“I understand that, but I think we should take a little more time. The DCNR ranger here has some leads. He’s trying to track down the cubs.”

“Two days, Cate. I’ll send your team ahead of you to Union County. It looks like we have a sow denned up near the Alvira Bunkers in State Game Lands 252. I have some cataloging the rest of your team can do until you arrive. Meet them there in two days.”

“I appreciate the extra time.”

Her boss harrumphed before disconnecting. Relief spread through her that she’d managed the telephone call without a full-fledged panic attack.

The deadline imposed by Virginia didn't bode well for the cubs' survival. If they could convince a game cop to get involved, there was a remote chance they'd find them in time. Certainly better than their odds if Malachi continued working the case alone. She earnestly prayed that it wasn't too late for the cubs.

BECKY DREW IN A deep breath and rubbed her shaky hands on her skirt. She could do this. The only way to make the change she hoped for come to pass was to eliminate Reece as an obstacle. And his own crimes would make it possible. Another deep breath and she pushed open the door to the park office.

It was him. This time she was certain. In her mind's eye she saw him as a child chasing butterflies in the outfield instead of catching baseballs. The strawberry mark on his neck gave him away. Not as vibrant as before, but it remained.

"I want to report a crime."

He raised an eyebrow. "What type of crime?"

Her gaze caught on a stuffed bear cub climbing a tree. Odd, she came here to discuss. Becky forced herself to turn away from the creature and instead stared at a park map pinned to a wall behind the desk. Inhaling the scent of burnt coffee, she folded her hands on top of the clutter-free counter to still them. "Selling wild bear cubs."

He ushered her into a back office and gestured for her to take a seat at a desk covered in paperwork. "Please tell me what you know."

"A man named Reece killed a bear and stole her three cubs."

"Who does he plan to sell them to?"

"I'm not sure, but he's meeting them at dusk tonight in the Loyalsock State Forest."

"Do you have an exact location?"

"No."

He frowned, reminding her of his father, Zeke, and a pang pierced her chest. His life was normal. Lonely, maybe, but a good one. He would make any parent proud, but here she was interfering with his well-ordered world. She should turn around and leave him alone. It was the right thing to do. Yet, she was incapable of doing that. Her own life depended on what happened here.

"If he's caught, will you arrest him?"

"It's more than likely he'll be fined."

"But not arrested?"

"He's unlikely to be arrested unless we can get him for something more." His sigh filled the small space. "I wish there were additional actions we could take against these offenders. We need stronger laws to protect the wildlife from people like him."

The problem arose from the possibility that without Reece's arrest, her plan would be unsuccessful. And once they caught him with the bear cubs, they'd be forced to leave the park. Even if the park rangers didn't evict them from their rental, there was no way Reece would stay after the authorities became aware of his presence. "The cubs are right here in the park."

"What did you say?"

"They're at the cabin where we're staying." She bit her bottom lip and rubbed her hands on her skirt. If he found out she'd told, he'd punish her. "Please don't tell him I'm the one who told you."

"How did this Reece manage to come across the bear's den? It wasn't on a marked trail, and it was well hidden."

"I'm not sure. I think I overheard something about a wildlife photographer leading him there."

"No name?"

"Sorry. He doesn't share much with me."

She tasted blood. Must've bitten her lip too hard. Nerves did that to her. There had to be a way to make sure Reece got locked up for his crimes. While the park rangers occupied him, she'd take the opportunity to search his stuff and see what she could dig up. The number of laws he'd broken over the years were too many to list. She might not have all the details, but people disappeared when Reece was around. All she required was some form of evidence. Then she could get him locked up and out of the way. She wasn't a fan of law-enforcement, but park rangers weren't so bad. If her son took custody of Reece, she wouldn't have to deal with the state police or the FBI. Even the thought of those agencies made her skin crawl.

The trouble would be getting into Reece's stuff without anyone noticing. But over the years she'd perfected the art of being invisible. She planned to put that skill to good use.

REECE LEANED AGAINST THE van, shaving wood off the block he held in his hand and watching as Byron tinkered with the engine on their VW bus. He did not have a knack for mechanics. He much preferred working with wood. Turning nothing into something. Creating fine things. Probably should've been a carpenter. He ran his thumb over the rough texture of the wood. A little sandpaper would smooth that right out. He'd fashioned after a bluebird. So delicate and sweet. His hands were capable of crafting beauty, even if destruction suited him better.

Choosing to work with wood wouldn't have been as financially rewarding as the career path he'd chosen, but it was a respectable means of earning a living. One without shame.

The clanging sound of the wrench ceased, and his friend pushed himself to his feet.

"You seen Becky around?" Reece asked.

"I've been kind of busy, but no." Byron's forehead creased as he wiped grease from his hands. He darted his gaze around and the nervous gesture did not go unnoticed. "Not in a couple of hours."

"Keep an eye out for her, will you?" He frowned. "Her demeanor has been different since we arrived in Pennsylvania. I want to know what changed."

"Sure thing." Byron threw down the rag and grabbed a bottle of water. "I'll watch her."

Chapter Six

Malachi's eyes widened when Becky pushed her shirt sleeves up.

"What happened?"

"Reece gave us bottles of milk and told us to feed the cubs."

The raised marks were scabbed over. He grimaced. "Those marks are from the cubs?"

"They are."

A different type of mark on her right palm caught his attention. "And what is that?"

"The cub mistook my hand for a pacifier."

It would've taken a great deal of suction to make a mark like that. "Looks painful."

"It's sore, but I'm fine."

"I'm going to need to take some pictures of your arms for the case file. Okay?"

She nodded, so he snapped a few photos of her arms and hands.

The scent of fresh coffee brewing, and the sound of his coworker, Kevin, bustling around reminded him of his manners. “Can I get you a cup of coffee or tea?”

Her gaze flicked to the door. “Nah. I need to get back before he notices I’m gone.” The words came out in a strangled whisper. “I need you to arrest him.”

Undoubtedly, she was afraid of this Reece fellow. What else had the man done to cause her such anxiety? Malachi wished he could reassure her an arrest would be made, and she’d be safe, but he wouldn’t lie. “If we catch him in the act selling wildlife parts or endangered species or something along those lines, we may be able to arrest him, but I’m afraid most crimes against wildlife don’t hold a lot of jail time. There are few exceptions.”

Becky bit her lip. She had a weird way of twisting her lip up and then chomping down like a crazed person, but he was certain he’d seen the action before. The gesture seemed strangely familiar. He averted his eyes and sucked in a breath.

Her name was Rebecca. No. It wasn’t her. Couldn’t be. His desire to see her again, to save her, was playing tricks on his mind. Her eyes were the same hazel color as his own, but it wasn’t all that unusual to have hazel eyes. This woman was not the one who gave him life. Her circumstances might match: group camping with an oddly charismatic leader. Probably a cult. Just like the vague memories from his early childhood.

He saw the similarities between the two women, and it was sad, but it didn’t mean a thing. His biological mother hadn’t been the only woman in the world taken in by false religion. And the name was common. Besides, she said her last name was Groves. His mother’s surname was James. Rebecca James.

This Becky had brought him useful information. He wasn't sure why she turned against her friend. Something was amiss in her circle of friends, but that wasn't his concern. It wasn't in his job description to mend relationships, and he wasn't sure where the strong urge to protect this woman came from. She'd unnerved him with her staring, and he wondered if she needed his help. There were missing pieces to her puzzle, but he didn't have time to invest in figuring out the mystery just because he had some irrational desire to protect this lady.

He had bear cubs that needed to be placed with a surrogate before they perished. Maybe while tending to that business, he'd find some way to help Becky.

Heading to the cabin before they had a chance to move the cubs was imperative, but first he'd call Cate with an update. No doubt she'd be thrilled to have a lead.

CATE TRIED TO IGNORE the strong chlorine smell as she paced beside Gavin's pool. The sunshine streamed into the room, giving the water a mirror-like appearance. She tried to puzzle out her next steps. There had to be something more she could do to rescue those missing cubs. The dark web sale turned out to be in Florida, and that made her think they weren't the cubs they were looking for. It was possible they'd been driven down there after being taken from the den, but it wasn't likely. They didn't have any other leads, and she'd soon be forced to give up trying.

Her cell buzzed and upon seeing Malachi's name flash across her screen she clicked to read his text.

Malachi: Busy?

Cate: No, but I only have two days to locate the cubs, then I need to be in Mount Pisgah. What are you up to?

Malachi: Cubs have been located. Are you able to take possession for the Game Commission?

Cate's shoulder's relaxed as she absorbed the welcome news.

Cate: Absolutely. I'll call dispatch and get a game warden to meet us. Where are we going?

Malachi: Here at Worlds End. Cabin rental. Number 7.

Cate: Wow. It takes guts to keep them on park property.

Malachi: Sure does. Woman who came in to report the crime claimed they were bottle feeding the cubs and the evidence on her arms leads me to believe her. Says she was forced to help. Has a hickey-like mark on her palm from one of the cubs.

Cate: They have razor-like claws, so it doesn't surprise me to learn they did damage. Hopefully, they didn't get too used to people. It won't serve them well in the long run if they've lost their fear of humans.

Malachi: What will you do with them?

Cate: We'll try to place them with denned sows who had their own cubs. They'll have to be separated since we can't place more than one in each den.

Malachi: The mama bears accept them?

Cate: We have tricks we use to help the mother bear believe they're her own.

Malachi: You've got me curious.

Cate: You should tag along and watch the process.

Malachi: Maybe I will. Meet me at the park office.

Cate: Forty-five minutes from now, okay?

Malachi: That'll work. I'll get eyes on the cabin to make sure they don't try to split with the cubs before we can scoop them up. According to the witness, this guy,

Reece, plans to sell them tonight, so we need to intercept them before that can happen.

Cate opened the solarium door and entered the dark hallway leading to the front rooms. She paused to send another message.

Cate: Maybe you should let the sale happen. That way, you can arrest the buyer and seller.

Malachi: It's short notice to set up. What if we make a mistake and lose the cubs?

Cate: I'm aware of the stakes and hate the idea of risking their lives, but I do want to see justice done.

She frowned as she grabbed her jacket from the closet by the door.

Cate: If we work together, we can make them pay and keep the cubs safe.

Malachi: You at your brother's house?

She slid her arms into her Carhartt jacket and waved to her sister-in-law to let her know she was leaving. Then sent a final text.

Cate: Yes. Putting on my coat now.

Malachi: See you when you arrive.

Chapter Seven

Becky rocked back and forth in the rocker by the front window of the cabin while she worked on the mending. Malachi hadn't come by to take the cubs, so they were still locked in one of the two bedrooms. She needed time alone to go through Reece's things and had hoped that when Malachi came, everyone would file outside giving her the chance to sneak in and look through the folder Reece kept in his laptop bag.

For the third time in as many minutes, Becky stabbed herself with the sewing needle. Her focus wandered to the flames dancing in the fireplace, and she set aside the skirt she'd been sewing. The children played too close to the hearth. If they were her kids, she'd correct them, but she no longer disciplined other people's children. And she wouldn't be having any more children of her own. She was the caretaker. Taught the younger girls how to do womanly things such as knitting, crocheting, and canning. She didn't have much of a formal education, but she'd learned the basics from the older women who'd been around back when Zeke ran things. Ezekiel James. Not a day went by when she didn't miss him. Her most recent letters to the prison had been returned undeliverable. If he'd been released, she didn't know where he'd gone. One day when Reece was out, she'd used his laptop and tried to find him, but the search had been fruitless.

The police called him a predator. But she'd loved him. He'd cared for her in a way nobody had since. When she'd given birth, he'd remained beside her throughout the entire process, placing a cool washcloth on her forehead. Giving her ice chips. Even cutting the cord before holding her and the babe close and telling her what a good job she'd done. He'd loved them. His wives may have been many, but he'd loved them each in their own way. And she knew he had a connection to God that nobody else had. It angered her that God had allowed him to be taken away from them. Why hadn't He warned him that the FBI was coming? It was hard to reconcile his connection with the Almighty with his ultimate imprisonment.

She would leave the community now if she could find out where he was and go back to him. If he would have her. She wasn't young anymore. And he liked young girls. Reece didn't believe in the same things Zeke had. He was against drugs, and women needed to be over eighteen to be entered into the community these days unless they were born into it. But he had his own vices. The man was far from saintly.

Dorcas scooped up Benjamin and shot Becky a disapproving look.

"The last time I corrected your kid, you went to Reece." Her mind went back to the week she'd spent being held in the isolation house. It was made of cinderblocks. In the West Virginia Appalachians, the cold seeped through the ground into one's bones. The thin sleeping bag given to her didn't do much to keep her warm. Provisions came once a day. Cold oatmeal and a canteen of water. A hole in the ground served as a bathroom. The stench became more than she could bear. She wouldn't go through that again. They'd been forced to flee the compound, so she didn't have to worry about that particular place, but knowing Reece, he'd find an equally disturbing punishment for community members who stepped out of line.

"I didn't mean to see you put in isolation. I only wanted him to remind you that you weren't in charge of our children."

"Reminder received."

"So, you were going to let my son fall into the fire?"

Becky shrugged. "Figured you'd stop gabbing with Eunice and notice before that happened." If she'd really thought the child was in danger, she would've done something, but Dorcas didn't need to know that. At least it wiped that incessant smile from her face.

The front door flew open, bringing a cold breeze inside along with Reece's imposing presence. He leaned down to kiss Dorcas, his blonde curls falling over his face as he did so. Then he turned to face Becky. His pale-blue eyes bore into her. "Where were you earlier?"

"Gathering firewood."

"There isn't much there. It couldn't have taken you more than ten minutes to gather it."

"I took a few minutes to enjoy the day."

"A storm is brewing. I feel it in my bones."

The sun was shining through the cabin windows, but she wasn't going to argue with him. His gaze turned to Dorcas and then Eunice. "Get these kids out from under my feet. Take them in the back room and keep them there until I say otherwise."

Becky wanted to ask when they would meet up with the rest of their community. She had a few friends left, but being here in Central Pennsylvania with only Reece, Byron, and their respective wives, Dorcas and Eunice and their children, made her feel completely alone and left out. This wasn't her family. It almost made her wish she'd never suggested they explore this area for their new compound. If it hadn't been her suggestion, he certainly wouldn't have insisted she join them here. Of course, if she hadn't come, she wouldn't have the opportunity to knock the crown from Reece almighty's head and give it back to the rightful heir. Her son.

The door opened again and Reece's brother, Byron, motioned for Reece to join him outside. She strained to hear what they were saying, and the few words she was able to catch sent tingles down her spine. They were going to leave the cabin before Malachi got there. All her planning had been for naught.

MALACHI SAT BESIDE CATE. They were parked cattywampus and half off the road, tucked behind a row of hemlocks and pines to obscure his truck from the sight-line of the cabin. Two men, including the one he'd checked in earlier that week, had been in and out no less than a dozen times in the past thirty minutes, but he couldn't figure out what they were up to.

Cate trained her binoculars on them as they continued their trips to and from their brightly colored Volkswagen bus. "I've never seen a VW bus in that shade of green before."

"Have you seen many of them?" he asked.

"Just a few. One was multi-colored. One was so rusted I couldn't tell its color."

He scratched the back of his neck. "Someone in Orangeville owns a powdered-blue. I've seen it a few times."

"Hmm. I'm not sure if lime green is better or worse than powder blue."

"It's a tough call." He tapped his fingers on the steering wheel. "Were you able to identify what they've been carrying?"

"Definitely not live animals, but that's about all I can tell you. Looks to me like they're packing up to leave. Probably checking out." She set down her binoculars. "I can't believe they had that much junk in a cabin that size."

A cloud covered the sun, turning the late afternoon gloomy, and the branches on the evergreens swayed erratically. "Looks like the weather is taking a turn," he said.

"I noticed that. They weren't calling for any precipitation, but with this wind, I'd be surprised if snow isn't on the horizon."

"You can taste it in the air. I'd be willing to bet on snow."

"I'm not taking that bet," she said.

"Are we all set for the stakeout?" he asked. "Hopefully this weather won't mess up our plans for tonight."

"Everything is lined up. We'll have two game cops backing us up."

"We driving together?" He preferred to drive himself places, but didn't want to sound chauvinistic by suggesting he drive.

"Might as well take separate cars. That way, we can use one of them to block one of the access roads, but we can sit together while we wait if you want."

Yes. He wanted. Stakeouts were less boring when you had

someone to talk to. And it certainly didn't hurt if that someone was easy on the eyes. "Sounds like a plan."

Chapter Eight

An inch of wet snow covered the roads as Cate wound her way through Loyalsock State Forest. The branches overhead formed a tunnel with snow raining down on her Ranger with every gust of wind. This night could turn treacherous, even deadly, if it ended in a chase.

Reaching the turnoff for High Knob overlook, she made the left onto Dry Run Road. While they couldn't be certain where exactly the exchange would take place, a forest ranger had noticed an unusual amount of activity near the overlook for this time of year. Cate hoped their impromptu task force was up to the challenge, and at least one of them would be in the right place to take down the poacher and the buyer. She'd asked Malachi to take a huge risk in not apprehending the poacher earlier, and now she prayed she hadn't made a monumental mistake. Second guessing herself wouldn't help anybody though.

Malachi. She saw his truck and pulled up beside him, putting down her passenger window so they could talk. "Ready?"

He hopped out and leaned into her window. "I know we had our strategy all worked out, but I'm thinking with this snow, we'd be risking our lives if we let them get near the overlook. Let's request barricades to block off Forest Road completely, so we don't end up with a high-speed chase that'll have anyone flying down the mountain."

It was something she should've thought of herself and probably would've if she hadn't been so busy questioning her choices. She nodded. "We could park down on McCarty and watch Dry Run Road from there."

"Sounds like a plan." He slapped her hood and got in his own vehicle then followed her down to McCarty. He used his truck to block the road, then hiked back and climbed in beside her with two insulated bags, which he set at his feet before taking out his radio. Icy pellets bounced off her windshield. "So much for the snow. Just what we need is ice. I'm going to check in with the forest guys, unless you already took care of it?"

She shook her head. "Figured you had a rapport with them." And she did not want him to witness her panic if she had to make the call herself.

He nodded and made the call. "You guys have some barricades handy?" After a brief conversation with his counterparts, he smiled. "They've got it covered. We should've sat in my truck. More head room."

"There are advantages to full-sized trucks, I suppose."

"With this weather, things could go south fast."

He was right. But the choice had been made, and they were here. A sigh escaped. "Tell me about it."

"We've got an hour before the exchange. I brought dinner."

How thoughtful. A smile tugged at her lips. "Is that what I smell?"

He opened the insulated bag and pulled out a sandwich for each of them. "They're Monte Cristos, but I don't know how well they held their heat." He handed her one.

She opened hers and took a bite. "It's still warm. This is fabulous. Thank you."

"You're welcome. The other bag has waters."

"You are an excellent stakeout partner. Do you know that?"

He chuckled. "I learned the hard way to be prepared."

"There has to be a story behind that." A gust of wind punctuated her statement.

His grin confirmed her suspicions.

MALACHI RUBBED HIS HANDS together to warm them. They alternated between running the engine to heat up the car and leaving it off to avoid wasting gas and so they could hear vehicles coming. Two cars had come down the road and both had turned around and left when they reached the barricades. Why anyone would choose a snowy day to visit the overlook, he couldn't say. Sometimes photographers did crazy things for the perfect picture, and he could almost understand their reasoning. But when your average person went out for a drive in dangerous conditions for no good reason, that made zero sense.

There was no way of knowing what the buyer was driving, but he expected Reece would show up in his hippie bus, which should make him easy to spot.

Cate turned slightly in her seat so she was facing him. "You're awfully quiet over there."

"I could say the same about you."

"I'm worried this thing will go south, and it'll be my fault that the bears don't wind up safe and sound since this stakeout was my idea."

"Don't do that. Yes, we want to get this guy Reece, but getting the buyer, too, makes sense."

"I guess. So, now you know what's been bothering me." She smiled. "What's your excuse for the silence?"

"It's the lady who gave us the information. Something about her is disturbing. And familiar."

"Familiar? How so?"

"I think she reminds me of my biological mother. That probably sounds crazy."

"Not at all." She tapped a short manicured fingernail on the console between them. "Were you adopted?"

"Foster care."

"How long?"

"From the time I was eight."

"Wow. That must've been hard." She frowned. "Do you mind if I ask why you were placed in foster care? Never mind. I don't want to overstep. You don't have to answer that."

He sighed. If anyone else had asked he probably wouldn't have answered. A succinct 'none of your business' would've sufficed, but there was something in the way she'd asked. A sincerity. Maybe he should answer her. What could it hurt? After she got her cubs, they'd probably never see each other again. No time for her to pity him. "My parents were part of a cult that was raided by the FBI."

"Raided? Why?" She bashed her head against the back of her

seat. "Sorry. I can't stop myself from asking nosy questions."

"It's all right. My father was the cult leader, and he took multiple wives. Younger wives. Illegal wives. Including my mother."

Her eyes shot open wide, and she covered her mouth.

He let out a mirthless laugh. "Yes. My father is a pedophile, and my mother was one of his victims. She was thirteen when she got pregnant with me. Fourteen when I was born. He was thirty-three."

"I'm so sorry. I cannot imagine how hard that must be for you."

"I've come to accept it, though I still wonder what ever happened to my mother." He stared straight ahead at the snow coming sideways. "We were brought to Pennsylvania because that was where my mother was raised, and I think she considered going to see her parents. Never did as far as I know. She stayed here for about a year after the cult disbanded, but then one night she left. There was a note saying she was going back to West Virginia. Life outside the community wasn't for her."

"She left you alone?"

"I wasn't alone. We stayed in a shelter for abused women. They contacted child services, and I was placed in foster care."

"Did you get placed with a good family?"

"I was shuffled around until I turned twelve. Then I was placed with my 'forever family.' That's what I call them. They're the ones who got me through my teenage years, sent me to college, and helped me to make something of my life."

"I'm glad you found them."

"It was a God thing. He knew I needed them, and maybe they needed me, too."

"I like that. God has a way of working things out for His purposes, doesn't He?"

"Yes. Even stakeouts. Look at that." He pointed. A white van, barely visible in the snow, made its way down the road. Noting the time on the dash, he sucked in a sharp breath of cold air. "It's time. That may be our buyer."

Chapter Nine

Before Cate had a moment to digest what Malachi told her, a van drove down the street, so she needed to keep her focus on the task at hand and not let herself become emotionally invested in the handsome park ranger seated beside her. Their relationship could never be more than a professional one. She didn't live nearby, and she traveled for work more often than she stayed put. No man in his right mind would want to get involved with a woman who was never around. As another vehicle pulled past them, she glanced beside her and lifted an eyebrow. "Should we follow?"

She knew he'd been expecting a different vehicle, but the group could've had more than one.

"I don't know. Could be them. Should we toss a coin?"

A laugh bubbled out of her. "Probably not. What does your gut tell you?"

He frowned. “Yeah. Go ahead. Follow.”

She slowly turned onto the road behind the sedan and kept a reasonable distance. Brake lights shone ahead of them, and she came to a stop as the sedan pulled in behind the van they’d seen earlier. It would be so much better if they could hear what the men said. “Want to call it in?”

Malachi nodded and lifted his radio. “Forest service will block off the road, and the Game Commission officers will join us here shortly. Wait until they arrive to approach.”

“Do you think that’s a good idea?” She heard the hitch in her voice. “What if they get away before the roadblock is in place?”

“No worries.” He grinned. “I have no intention of following my own advice.” His door opened without warning, and he was trudging through the snow to reach the stopped vehicles.

Before she could think through what she was doing, she hopped out of her truck and followed him. She was carrying. Her brothers insisted she learn how to shoot and get her conceal carry permit after what happened with the Continental Alliance, but she didn’t like guns and prayed she’d never have to aim it at a person.

Malachi was silent up ahead. Snow smacked Cate in the face and stuck to her eyelashes, making it hard to see him in the shadows of the tree line. It was clear he was attempting to remain hidden until he could hear what they were up to and determine if this was the exchange they were awaiting. A blast of wind whipped through her coat, and she folded her arms against the cold.

A child’s screams tore through the night, and she hurried to Malachi’s side. “What on earth?”

“I don’t know.” Malachi stepped out into the open with his badge and gun drawn and rapped on the window of the van.

He identified himself when the driver rolled down his window. Cate remained a few steps behind him, prepared to assist if anything should go awry.

The words that came from the car left her stomach clenched in knots.

“My wife doesn’t want me coming to her house where her new boyfriend lives. I meet her here to drop off my son.” The poor kid. A pawn in the middle of his parents’ games. But not the reason they were there.

“All right. Get a move on. We have an operation in progress, and you got in the middle of it.” Malachi let out a heavy sigh.

“Oh. Sorry.”

When the van pulled out, she released her pent-up breath. “That was an epic fail.”

“Definitely didn’t go as expected. Better let the others know they can let these bozos through.”

Static on the radio stopped any further conversation. The only words Cate caught were ‘in pursuit.’

Once back in her truck, they looked into each other’s eyes. The pursuit could be the poacher or the buyer. Or even both. She needed to get those cubs into the custody of Game Commission where they could be protected. And if this operation failed, she only had herself to blame. Then her thoughts went to the game cops chasing the suspects. If they were injured, she couldn’t live with herself.

“Let’s head back to my truck. While you drive, I’ll call on my cell and hopefully get a better connection to find out who their pursuing and why.”

MALACHI STARTED HIS TRUCK and pulled out. He'd received confirmation that Ted Stevens, a Game Commission officer assisting them on the stakeout, had taken off after a suspect who fled the scene when the guy spotted him. Malachi's nerves were on edge, and he clenched his teeth as he tried to contain his frustration with the risk the officer had taken in choosing to pursue a suspect in these conditions. The last thing he needed was for this to go poorly.

If he hadn't been so charmed by Cate, he never would've agreed to wait when the cubs were in a far more easily controlled environment from the start. It was a mistake. A big one. He couldn't blame her though. She wasn't law-enforcement. Her knowledge of how these things worked probably came from her bodyguard brothers and television shows where cops always chose the high-risk, high-reward paths.

He looked at his speedometer. 45 mph. Far too fast for conditions, but a game cop's life was at stake, and he wouldn't hesitate to risk his own to help his fellow officer.

The unearthly grinding wail of metal colliding against metal had him tapping his brakes. A man stumbled from a gray SUV that had collided with a DCNR vehicle, flipping it on its side and reversing the way it was facing. Once the guy got his bearings, he ran down the road. A compact car reversed full speed, and before Malachi had time to do more than jump from his truck and sprint toward the crash, the fleeing suspect had jumped into the car and disappeared around a curve. Cate's truck pulled up as he approached the driver's side of the DCNR truck. The driver didn't respond when he tapped on the window. The door wouldn't open. He looked back at Cate. "There's a window cutter in the emergency kit in the backseat of my truck."

She hurried to his truck, while he continued to look for a way into the vehicle. The passenger door was crushed in, but the window was broken. It would be a challenge to pull Stevens through the window on the steep incline. Cate returned, and he met her at the driver's window. He broke the glass and brushed it away, hoping he wouldn't cut Ted in the process. Then he released the man's seatbelt, praying for a miracle.

"Will he be all right?" Cate voiced the question buzzing in his own mind.

He took off his jacket, ignoring the icy chill as fat flakes continued their assault. Malachi laid the coat on the ground then pulled the other man through the window and set him down on it. His forehead was bleeding, and airbag burns and seatbelt marks would do their share of damage, too, but despite the injuries they caused, they likely saved his life. He tried to warm his fingers by rubbing them together to get some of the feeling back before placing them to check the man's pulse. He blew out a relieved breath when he found one. "I don't know. But I'm hopeful." Sirens announced the arrival of EMS, and he gladly stepped back allowing them to take over. He moved to the gray SUV. A Ford Explorer. Three sets of tiny black eyes stared up at him from a dog crate resting on the passenger seat, but it wasn't puppies inside the crate. "Cate, come here, please."

Chapter Ten

Donny, the man he'd trusted enough to sell the bear cubs to, stared straight ahead as the snow continued to fall. His grip on the steering wheel was tight enough to turn his knuckles white. Reece sat beside him cracking his neck.

Something had gone terribly wrong. Law-enforcement had known about the exchange. Someone in his inner circle would pay for the breach. So would the buyer. You couldn't be too careful.

"Where are you driving?" Reece asked.

"I guess wherever you want to go."

If he was an undercover, he could be trying to find out where Reece was staying. Looking to gather evidence to prove he was into more than wildlife trafficking. That wasn't going to happen. If they figured out who he was, he'd be going away for the rest of his life. Might even get the death penalty. Taking the man's life was preferable to taking the chance he might prove to be a problem in the future. Maybe he could let him go. He might not even be the leak. Probably wasn't. No. He had to go. Donny would have to die. It was a shame, but a necessary evil.

The car slipped on the snow-covered road and Donny quickly righted their course, but it brought on a flash of the wreckage they'd left behind. Had the cop survived? Unlikely.

When they'd driven for about ten minutes, Donny sighed. "Do you mind telling me what happened back there?"

"I was hoping you could tell me." Reece grabbed his pistol and held it to the other man's head. "Pull over up ahead."

CATE TUGGED ON A pair of thick elbow-length gloves. They were rough against her skin and always made her think of the one's falconers wore when working with birds of prey. Malachi loaded the crate into her truck and hurried over to the ambulance. Pulling out one of the bear cubs, she did a quick examination by headlamp.

In anticipation of finding them, she had lined up a wildlife rescue that could keep the cubs until they found adoptive mothers for them, but she wasn't sure she'd be able to bring them by this late. Her team had one sow lined up to receive the first of the cubs, but the other two would need to wait until they located suitable adoptive mothers. One seemed smaller and weaker than the other two, so they'd place her first in hopes of giving her a better chance for survival.

Her eyes flicked toward the ambulance as it rode away with Ted Stevens on board. Pausing in her ministrations, she closed her eyes briefly and lifted up a prayer for the officer and his family. Then she forced her focus back to the job at hand, pushing all other thoughts from her mind.

A touch to her shoulder startled her, and her breath caught as she looked over her shoulder into Malachi's warm gaze.

"Just checking on you and your charges," he said. His deep voice had a calming effect on her rattled nerves and made her almost wish this wasn't the end of her assignment here.

"I think they'll be all right."

"And you?"

"Not thrilled with the way things went tonight. I'm sorry I kept you from stopping them earlier. I hope you can forgive me."

"It was my decision to make, Cate. What happened here tonight was not your fault."

Not reassuring at all. Now she hadn't only pushed him into making an unwise decision, he planned to take the full force of the weight of that choice onto his shoulders. That only made her stomach clench tighter, but she forced a smile. "Nevertheless, it feels like it was."

"Wish I could convince you otherwise."

"These little ones must be freezing without their mother here to provide heat. I'd better get going if I'm going to get them placed tonight. I don't think my brother would be thrilled if I brought them to his house."

He chuckled. "I'm not sure my dog would be happy either, but if you need somewhere to keep them for the night, you can bring them to my place."

"I'm going to head back to the park office and make some calls from there. Join me?" she asked.

His eyes searched hers, but she couldn't guess what he was

hoping to find there.

WHEN BYRON HELD THE passenger door open, Becky slipped out of the vehicle and sank into the mud. Yesterday's early morning snow had melted, leaving a mess behind. Her gaze took in her new surroundings as she steadied herself against the van. Their new home. A clearing in the midst of the woods. A large enough area for all ten cabins if they stayed there, but she knew they wouldn't remain here long.

It was state land, which made it a temporary stop. Soon enough they'd move onto private land somewhere.

Reece wouldn't buy a plot of land. He refused to do that. As far as he was concerned, land couldn't be owned, so he would look for abandoned houses with acreage. At least that's what Eunice told Priscilla she'd overheard from Reece and Byron. Becky preferred firsthand information, but that required greater risk than using Priscilla to get it for her.

Later that same night, she sat around the campfire with the rest of the group. Smoke blew in her direction, and she waved it off so she could breathe. Their community was together again, most of them having arrived at Loyalsock State Forest shortly before Byron and Becky got there. Coyotes called out to each other in the distance. Their calls sent chills running down her spine.

The hum of approaching vehicles caused her shoulders to tense until she saw two familiar campers. One for Reece, Dorcas, and their kids. The other for Byron, Eunice, and their children. The rest of them would stay in tents for now. Several men got to work setting them up.

"I've got your tent ready, Becky."

Clarence. If she hadn't given Zeke her whole heart, she'd have fallen for him.

"Thanks." She stood and followed him to the semi-secluded area where she'd live for the time being.

He lingered instead of rejoining the group.

"Something on your mind?" she asked.

"You." His smile was tinged with sadness. "Zeke is out of prison."

"I know."

"He's not coming back."

"How do you know that?"

He surveyed the area before meeting her gaze. "While Reece and Byron were away, I looked him up. He found God."

"That's not new. He talked to God all the time."

"No. Zeke's different. He was spouting off stuff about being born again and being washed in the blood. He's not the same man he was back then."

A gust of wind reminded her that she'd be sleeping alone in a cold tent tonight. She bit her lip. "I've been wondering about Ezekiel, but maybe Malachi can take his place. He's his son. Our rightful leader if Zeke isn't coming back."

"He had many sons."

"I was head wife. That makes my son the next in line." Her mind flashed back to a time when she was content. Her child on her hip. The jade around her neck.

"Why was it all right for him to have multiple wives, but you won't accept a new husband even now that he's been gone for twenty-four years?"

"I tried, Clarence. We tried. They told me it was for the good of the community, so I accepted you. But we didn't produce any children, so I stopped trying. If we were supposed to be together, God would've given us babies."

"Do you even hear yourself?" He shook his head. "At some point you need to realize that nothing they've told us is true. We could leave here. Have a real life together like outsiders do."

"You can go. I won't say a word to anyone, but I can never leave here. Have a normal life. I tried and failed ... left my only son behind. Now he's part of that world." She frowned. "But I can never go back."

His brow furrowed. "If I help you get Reece and Byron out of the way, so you can get Malachi to take Zeke's place, will you finally accept me as your husband?"

Her voice shook as she answered. "I'm married to Ezekiel."

"There is no paperwork, Rebecca. You're free to marry another."

"Once I hear from him that he refuses to return to the community, I'll consider your offer, but I can't promise more than that."

"Then it'll have to be enough." He pulled her to him and kissed the top of her head.

She let herself revel in the warmth of his embrace for a moment before stepping out of his arms. The comfort he promised held its appeal, but her mission was larger than the two of them. What needed to be done was for the good of the community. "We have a lot of work to do."

CHAPTER ELEVEN

BACK AT THE OFFICE, Malachi wrestled the cub into a position that kept him mostly still to feed him his bottle. The male cub he held had soft, dense fur and was larger than the other two. Satisfied mewling sounds echoed through the office as he took his fill. Cate had enlisted his help with the task, and he now knew without a doubt how Becky had gotten the deep scratches on her arms.

"That kneading motion is how they encourage the mother to produce more milk."

"Doesn't it hurt her?"

She shook her head, smiling. "No. She's built for it. Unlike us. You should've worn the gloves."

"And look like a wimp in front of a pretty woman?" Warmth flooded his cheeks, and he turned away to avoid her gaze. He hadn't meant to say that out loud. His filter was sorely lacking.

"Pretty, huh? Do you say that to all your colleagues?"

"I think this is a first." He shook his head. "And I shouldn't have said it. Sorry."

"Why? Didn't you mean it?"

Oh. This girl was trouble. She was going to be the death of him. Not only had he let her talk him into making a poor decision, now his professionalism was all but gone, and he hadn't a clue how to respond.

"I meant it. No harm in telling you that now, I guess. We won't be working together after tonight."

"I guess that's true unless you do come along when we place the first cub. We tentatively scheduled our visit to the den in Union County for Friday morning. It's a little over an hour from here."

"I'm on the schedule, but I might be able to get someone to switch shifts with me."

"It'll be rewarding to see her snuggled up to her adoptive mom, getting fed properly once more." Cate put the bear cub back into the crate. "I'm going to try once more to reach the rescue. If not, I'll just stay here with them until they open."

"What about food? Do you have enough with you?"

She tested the milk on her arm and then pulled the gloves on before reaching for the final cub. "I brought enough bear milk replacer and mush for them."

"I meant for you."

"There may be a granola bar in my truck."

"Come back to my place."

She reached for the bottle on the counter and turned it slowly, keeping her focus on the spinning bottle. "That wouldn't be appropriate, Malachi."

"I'm not propositioning you, Cate. I'm offering a safe place for you and the cubs to spend the night. I have a spare room you can use. The cubs can have the pantry. It's heated."

She hesitated, then nodded. "Okay."

"You're not afraid of enormous dogs, are you?"

There was a glint in her eyes when they widened. "Love them."

CATE RAISED AN EYEBROW when Malachi kept his hand on the knob after unlocking the front door. "Everything okay?"

"I've tried to train him not to jump, but he gets excited on the rare occasion we have company, but if you sit right down, he'll likely put his head on your lap and let you pet him without knocking you over.

"Don't worry about me." She grinned. "Let me at him."

He swung the door open and a giant black, white, and rust-colored dog jumped on the glass storm door. She let herself in and knelt to the dog's level, burying her face in his soft fur. "Aren't you a beauty?" She cooed at him while petting him.

"Cate, meet Titan." He scanned the living area. "Pixie is here somewhere."

"Titan and Pixie?" She laughed. "Cute. Is Pixie a poodle?"

He darted his gaze around the room. "She's my cat. Probably hiding on top of the refrigerator. She's not as fond of company as Titan is."

"You don't strike me as a cat person." She surveyed the area hoping to spot her.

"I'm not, but she decided to adopt me. I didn't get much say in the matter." He chuckled. "She showed up one day and never left. And she's grown on me."

She stood and brushed dog hair from her slacks and glanced back at her truck. "Is there another way into the pantry, so we don't have to bring the bear cubs past Titan?"

"No, but he's a good boy. He'll get in his crate if we ask nice."

Once the dog was secured, Malachi wrestled the crate through the house and deposited it in the pantry area. Cate squatted and watched as the three cubs snuggled up together, their bellies full from their earlier meal. This was her dream job, and she was grateful to be doing it. Having colleagues like Malachi made it even sweeter, but leaving wouldn't be easy. She'd see him Friday, but after that it could be a long time before they ran into each other again. It might never happen. Part of her wanted to make the most of the time they had left and get to know him better, but another part wanted to wall herself off to keep safe from the heartbreak that was sure to come if she let him in.

The room was larger than Cate's kitchen and lined with linoleum tile. "I was expecting a small area filled with canned goods when you said it was a pantry."

"There's some canned cat food up there." Malachi's gaze traveled to the top shelf where a Munchkin cat with a tabby coat peered down on them, her golden eyes laced with suspicion.

She made noises to encourage the cat to come closer, but the feline didn't move from her perch, so Cate turned her attention back to Malachi. "Never saw so many blank shelves outside of grocery stores at the start of the pandemic." They lined three of the four walls and the only thing on them was a thin layer of dust.

"Ha ha. I have food on the shelves in the kitchen. It's only me, so I'm not shopping in bulk at Sam's Club," he said.

"In that case, you can make dinner. I'm starved."

MALACHI GRABBED A BAG of frozen stir-fry vegetables from his freezer and added some to the pan sizzling on the stove. Honey-garlic chicken and vegetables. There were few dishes he could make in a flash that were as delicious as they were quick and easy. This was one of them.

"Smells spicy." Cate joined him in the kitchen.

"Do you like your food with a little kick, or should I make it milder?" He stirred the concoction.

"I'm sure it'll be fine the way you usually make it." She leaned back against his counter and made eye contact. "Can I help with anything?"

"You could set the table." He showed her where the plates and silverware were kept.

"Minute rice?"

"You said you were starving, so I didn't think you'd want to wait for me to make rice the old-fashioned way."

She smiled. "You were right."

Once the rice sat for five minutes, he fluffed it with a fork, then put the meal together in a serving bowl. He wouldn't have bothered with the extra dish if he'd been eating alone, but for some reason he wanted everything to be perfect for Cate.

After carrying the food to the table, he sat down beside Cate and took her hand. Her eyes searched his. He grinned. "I'm going to ask the blessing on our meal."

"Okay." A pink hue tinged her cheeks, making him wonder if it was his touch affecting her or if she was uncomfortable with prayer.

"Father, thank you for this meal and for the abundance of blessings you've showered us with. Please guide us and protect us. Be with Cate as she finds homes for the bear cubs and please let the new moms accept them. In Jesus' holy name we pray. Amen."

"Amen." Cate looked up at him. "Thank you for praying for me and the cubs."

"Of course." He scooped up a forkful of rice and chicken. "Dig in before the food gets cold."

Her plate was empty mere minutes later, and she pushed it away. "That was delicious."

"Glad you enjoyed it. Have a second helping."

"No. I'm stuffed." She rested her hand on her stomach. "I'll take care of the dishes."

"You're my guest. I'll handle them. Then I'll show you to your room so you can get some rest."

Chapter Twelve

Emmett Reed was standing at the counter when Cate pushed her way through the double doors into the wildlife rehab center. She glanced around the room and took a quick stock of the cages in the front room. There was a raccoon, an owl, a rabbit, and a domestic cat.

"Hey, Cate. How's it going?"

"It's all good." She cocked her head to the side. "What's with the house cat?"

"The elderly man who brought it in thought it was a bobcat."

"Did he wear glasses?"

He chuckled. "As a matter of fact, he did. And he promised to visit his eye doctor to see if his prescription needs to be updated. The feline is chipped, and her family is on their way to pick her up."

"All's well that ends well, I guess." She shook her head and smiled, then waved her hand toward the door. "Any chance you can give me a hand?"

His eyes widened. "You brought the bear cubs?"

"I did. And they're all in a single crate, so it's not light."

He shuffled out from behind the counter and joined her as she went out to her truck. Together they lugged the crate inside and released their captives into a much larger pen area. "Thanks for bringing them by."

"We'll be back for the tiny one on Friday morning."

"Didn't you name them?"

"I'm not supposed to name them. You know that. We're not supposed to form attachments to them or encourage them to form attachments to us."

"Doesn't mean you listened." He was right. She imagined the girls being named Itsy and Bitsy and the boy, Bruce. But she kept her names to herself. "I better skedaddle. See you in a couple of days."

Emmett walked her to the door. "Take care, Cate."

When she settled back into her driver's seat, she had an overwhelming urge to shut her eyes, but fought it off. She found a satellite station playing Alison Krauss and turned up the volume. The woman's voice had an ethereal quality to it she wished she could match. Once she got home and collected her cat, she could relax. Right now, she needed to keep her exhaustion at bay, and music paired with a cracked window to let in fresh air helped her fight it.

Malachi entered the recently vacated rustic log cabin

and turned in a slow circle. Didn't appear they'd left anything behind, but it hadn't been cleaned yet, so he had to check.

The billing address and phone number they'd given when booking the reservation didn't appear to be valid. This case might be one of the many that went unsolved. Without a way to track the group, he was at a loss. No social media profile for Becky or Rebecca Groves.

Something gnawed at the edges of his mind. West Virginia. His biological father's community had been located in the wilds of West Virginia. Reece had a West Virginia accent. It was not outside of the realm of possibilities. Not likely, granted, but it was possible Reece could've resurrected the cult.

Kevin smacked his gum as he entered the cabin. "Find anything?"

"I walked in two seconds before you."

"So, that's a no?" Kevin scratched his head.

He shook his head and headed into the back rooms. Kevin was a nice kid. Smart as a whip when it came to genus and species. Even had a knack for technology. His lack of common sense irked Malachi.

Nothing. The rooms were all empty save the musty smell he imagined came from the bear cubs. A park map was pinned to one wall though. He strolled over to it. Something shiny on the windowsill caught his eye, and he reached for it and ran his fingers over the smooth, cool surface of the jasper stone. It dangled from a cord. Familiar. A flash hit him of his mother sitting on a cot in the women's shelter, running her fingers over a similar gem. She'd told him his father had given it to her because she was his favorite wife. Second in command. His other wives were only identified from their simple gold rings. Pushing the memory aside, he refocused on the map. An area outside of the park boundaries—near where the bear-cub exchange had taken place—was circled. That was probably why it was circled, but it couldn't hurt to look into it further. He pulled out the thumbtacks holding it to the logs and a slip of paper fell to the floor.

From mountain heights to shadows deep, your strength is found in what you keep. Uncover the roots of the past for in them your future is cast.

She'd meant for him to find the note and the stone. What little doubt he'd had dissipated in an instant. Becky Groves was his biological mother. He closed his eyes and focused on his breathing. Why the cryptic message? She'd been in his office days earlier. Why not open up then? Forcing his tight jaw to loosen, he considered his next steps. He owed her nothing. But the fear in her eyes and those shaking hands hadn't been for show. Regardless of what she'd done to him, she was a vulnerable woman in a bad situation. And he wasn't sure he could turn his back on her.

Kevin knocked on the door frame. "You all right in here?"

"Just peachy." He unclenched his fist and stuffed the stone into his pocket as he turned to face his coworker. "Call in the cleaning crew, will you? They left this place smelling like a zoo."

The young park ranger tapped his hat. "Sure thing."

CATE ARRIVED HOME AND stopped by her landlady's place to pick up her cat before going inside. She rented an apartment above Maggie's garage. At her knock, Maggie smiled and ushered her into the house.

"I'll make some tea."

"That'd be lovely." Cate bent and picked up Penny. The calico purred in welcome and nuzzled her chin. She smiled against her soft fur. A few seconds passed before the cat jumped down to investigate her food bowl.

Cate waited in the doorway between the dining room and kitchen. "Aren't you supposed to be retired?" She gestured to the dining table strewn with worn textbooks along with a few true crime novels.

"I am, but I was invited to guest lecture. The new religion professor is going to be out of town for a few weeks."

"Do you use the true-crime stories in your classes?"

"I do, yes. Reading a few passages from one of those captivates young minds more than the sterile writing in their textbooks."

"Maybe I'll sit in. Heard the new guy is an atheist."

"That he is. Which gives me the opportunity to encourage his students to think for themselves. Investigate and form their own conclusions."

"Hope you have success." She pulled out a kitchen chair and sat.

"You look troubled, hon."

"We placed a bear cub with an adoptive mother this morning. Her own mom was killed by poachers a few days back."

"It's wonderful that you were able to place her, so why are you so glum?"

"I'll sound like a lovesick teenager if I tell you."

"You met someone?"

"Maybe. I don't know." Penny leapt into her lap, and she stroked her soft fur. "He's great, but he lives a couple of hours from here, so nothing can come of it."

"Don't be so sure about that." Maggie poured the tea and set out a jar of local honey along with a teaspoon. "God has a way of working things out."

"I suppose you're right. My faith is on shaky ground lately."

"I've had seasons in my life when I placed my hope in worldly things, but even when I got what I wanted it never gave me any satisfaction. Only God can make sense of our troubles. We must focus on spiritual things rather than carnal." Maggie made eye contact as she added honey to her mug. "You need to spend time with God if you want to mend your relationship with Him."

She stared at the liquid swirling in her mug as she stirred it. "It's not as if I stopped believing."

"Come to services with me Sunday morning."

Cate lifted the stoneware mug and took a tiny sip of her tea, testing the temperature. Too hot. She knew she should be attending a local church, but she hadn't since she'd started school. It was far easier to forgive others than it was to forgive herself. Mistakes she made in the past cost her friends dearly, and it was hard to put them behind her.

Chapter Thirteen

MALACHI FROWNED AT HIS laptop. He was looking for information on his biological father and the community he'd led, known simply as 'Jade.' He would've expected to find more—had found more the last time he'd searched—but some of the links to articles he'd bookmarked no longer worked.

On a whim, he'd tried Rebecca James, too. Not that he'd expected much. It had been ten years since he made his last attempt to look up his mom. Nothing new turned up, just the same articles from when his father was arrested, and the cult broken up.

"Jade?" Kevin's voice spoke from behind him, and he minimized the search window. He hadn't heard him approach. The kid had skills. He'd make an excellent stalker. Shaking off the disturbing thought, he grabbed his cup and stood to refill it.

"It's nothing."

"If you're trying to get more information about them, I can help."

There was no arguing that. The kid was better at finding things online than Malachi was, but did he want him digging around in his past? Not really. Malachi filled his mug and faced Kevin. "All right." It was work-related, and he couldn't ignore the connection despite his strong desire to do just that. "See what you can find about them. I think the poacher might've restarted that community. Possibly with a new name."

"How did you make that connection?"

He took a sip of his bitter brew and debated lying, but couldn't do so in good conscience, so he reached into his pocket and wrapped his fingers around the cold stone. Some things couldn't be hidden. Pulling it from his pocket he tossed it to Kevin. "It was left in the cabin."

"A gemstone pointed you in that direction? Sounds like a leap."

"It may be." He could be wrong, but it wasn't likely. His past had come back to haunt him, and now he had to expose it to the light.

Kevin sat at his own computer. "I'll let you know what I find."

Less than thirty minutes later as Malachi was reading a recent article about his biological father's release from prison, Kevin let out a strangled sound.

"You look just like him."

Malachi sighed but said nothing. Not what he expected. He'd figured Kevin would find articles, but he hadn't counted on the pictures. Yes, he did look like Ezekiel James.

"Is he your father, Malachi?"

No sense in denying it. The pictures spoke for themselves.

"Use that big brain of yours and figure it out, Kev."

"No need to get snippy. I'm trying to help."

"Sorry. I shouldn't have snapped at you, but I never expected this to be something I'd be forced to share with my coworkers." He scrubbed a hand across his face. "His name is Ezekiel. Mine is Malachi. You know I grew up in foster care. I made the connection to the Jade."

"So, he is."

"Yes. Ezekiel James is my biological father. And there may be a connection to the poacher-turned-wildlife trafficker who stayed in cabin seven." No need for Kevin to know that the connection was Malachi's own mother. His privacy had been compromised enough for one day. Some things should remain buried in the past.

CATE LOOKED AT PENNY sleeping so peacefully atop her lap. She hated to disturb her, but she needed to eat dinner soon. A knock at the door solved the problem for her as Penny hopped down, so she could properly hide from their company. Cate peered out her window before opening the door wide. "To what do I owe this unexpected visit?"

"Is that any way to greet your brother?"

She shook her head and rolled her eyes then hugged Grayson's wife, Jenna. "It's good to see you both. But what are you doing here?"

"We were in the area, so thought we'd stop by."

"Come on in. I'll make some tea. If I drink coffee now, I'll be up all night. I can make some for you though, if you want."

"Water will do. Thanks, sis."

"I'll help you make the tea." Jenna followed her into the tiny kitchen.

"I'm not buying that you two were in the area, so what's going on?" Cate filled a pot with water and set out two mugs.

Jenna grabbed the box of chamomile tea and put a bag in each cup. "Gavin called him about some guy you're supposedly seeing."

Cate let out a huff. "I knew it. The two of them refuse to let me take care of myself."

Her sister-in-law placed a hand on her shoulder. "I tried to talk him out of showing up here, but we were in the area. Sort of. A new client wanted a face-to-face."

"How close were you?"

"Forty-five-minute drive."

She forced a smile. "I guess I should expect him to drop by when he's that close, but he could've called first."

Jenna laughed. "I told him to, but I think he was hoping to find the guy here so he could kill him."

Cate shook her head again. "I'm not seeing anyone. I went out for a single dinner with a colleague. It wasn't a date." She poured the water into the cups, releasing the scent of chamomile into the air. "How did he even know about my dinner?"

Jenna giggled and tilted her head to the side.

"Gavin told him. Of course, he did."

"But you like him." Jenna's eyes widened. "It's written all over your face. This guy means something to you."

"It doesn't matter. There is no way it could work. He lives over by Worlds End. I'm here. Geography isn't on our side." Besides, he wouldn't want to get involved with a girl so emotionally challenged. He knew nothing about what she'd been through. Her captivity had changed her inside. She wasn't the same sweet girl she'd been before the Continental Alliance had impacted her life.

Jenna chuckled. "It wasn't on our side, either. Nor was it on Gavin and Samantha's side."

"Malachi isn't wealthy, he can't pick up his life and move the way Gavin did."

"True, but you are. And you can." Jenna glanced around the tiny flat. "You might choose to live like a pauper, but if you wanted to, you could follow that guy to the ends of the earth."

"He doesn't even know who my daddy is. No reason to bring it up with someone I'm not dating." Cate took a sip of tea. "Besides, if I were dating him, my brothers would definitely be a problem."

"Trust me when I tell you, they already are." Jenna made eye contact with Grayson who filled the doorway to her tiny kitchen with his presence. He scowled at her in his playfully menacing way. Cate's college friends used to say he looked like Reacher on the television show. Cate didn't see it, but his size definitely compared.

CATE CURLED UP ON the couch and covered herself with her faux fur weighted blanket. Running her fingers through the soft fur, she smiled to herself. Her brothers were a royal pain, but they loved her and would do anything to keep her safe.

She grabbed her teacup from where she'd set it on the coffee table and inhaled the fragrant steam before taking a long sip. Her brothers had quite the scare a couple of years prior when she'd disappeared from school, so she understood their overprotectiveness to an extent, but they'd ventured into the extreme if they thought they had a right to screen her dates.

"It's good to see you, Katydid."

"I hate it when you call me that."

"No, you don't. You love it."

She couldn't hold back a smile. Truth be told, she did like it. It reminded her of her mother. That was what she'd called her, and Grayson had taken to using the nickname after Mom's death.

"I'm glad you're here. How was Disney?"

"Not bad. Trina liked the princess castle."

Jenna smiled. "We bought her a princess dress to wear. Want to see pictures?"

Cate nodded, and Jenna pulled them up on her cell.

When they were finished browsing through the photos, Gray narrowed his eyes and steepled his hands together on his lap. "Now, tell me more about this Malachi James."

"Not much to tell." Penny hopped up beside her, and Cate lifted her to her face. "Finally, resigned to having company?" She kissed the top of her head and set her on her lap and the cat did a few circles before lying down. Within seconds she was purring. There were many days when Penny had been her lifeline. On days when she hadn't wanted to get out of bed, she'd risen simply to care for the cat. If she hadn't been there, her spiral wouldn't have been as short-lived as it was.

"My research into him shows he didn't exist in the system until he was eight."

"I assumed as much." Cate chuckled. "And you shouldn't be researching my coworkers without asking me first."

Jenna gave her a high five, and Gray frowned. "Why would you assume such a thing?"

"He told me he'd been born into a cult. It's not uncommon for them not to visit hospitals and get all the proper paperwork when children are born."

"Where did you learn so much about cults?"

"I watched some documentaries and took a class in school."

"Before or after your run-in with the Continental Alliance."

"After."

He nodded. "Yeah. I wouldn't necessarily call them a cult, but a secret society with religious underpinnings is close enough to one. I can see why you would want to learn more to protect yourself in the future."

"I think it was more about being able to identify that kind of manipulation if I ever saw it again. If something like what happened with Emmaline and Brittany ever arose again, I hope I would be able to recognize it and prevent it." And she wouldn't be fooled into trusting a man simply because he was her father's friend. These days, she looked deeper before putting her faith in someone.

"I'm not sure it would be that easy to keep anyone else safe. People are going to do what they want even if their loved ones warn them about the dangers."

"You may be right." She drew in a steadying breath and made eye contact. "There is a subject I'd like to broach with you. I don't want you and Gavin checking out guys for me unless I specifically request that you do."

Jenna smiled and nodded. "You tell him."

Gray gave his wife a stern look, and she held up her hands in surrender.

"That is a request I'm not certain I'm willing to honor."

“I need you to let me make my own mistakes.”

“After what happened to you the last time you decided to keep us in the dark, you should want to keep us informed.”

“And if I need your help, I’ll tell you.”

“I’m taking a job in Williamsport, so I’ll only be an hour away if you need me.”

“I won’t need you.” As the words passed her lips, she hoped she wouldn’t regret them.

Chapter Fourteen

Friday morning, Malachi trudged along beside Cate and her team on the wide snow-covered path leading to the Alvira Bunkers. They passed the ruins from an old church on the right just before reaching a cemetery. You could just make out the federal prison in the distance. He slowed his steps as he neared an enormous tree, its branches glittering with ice. Its beauty undeniable, strangely contrasted with the history of the place. So many people had been displaced when the government took their land, claiming eminent domain.

He veered off the path and approached a memorial to a union soldier, brushed the wintry mix off the cold metal, and traced the inscription. He'd researched the site before making the trip. The town of Alvira had been purchased during World War II for their munitions factory, or so the story went. Now it was part of State Game Lands 252.

A short time later, they arrived at the bunker a black bear sow was using as a den site. The echo of her mewling cubs confirmed they were in the right place. It was a safe, dry place to spend the winter, but he wondered what would happen when the weather turned warmer. Hopefully, curious explorers would stay away until the space was once again empty.

The game warden, Jack Carter, positioned himself in the doorway and shot the sow with a tranquilizer gun. After a few minutes to be sure she was out, the team moved inside and got to work.

Malachi glanced around at the graffiti covering the interior of the bunker and shook his head. Human hands could do so much. They'd built this place, and now they desecrated it. He blew out a breath and stood to the side, watching the group work.

They checked the sow's radio collar and replaced the flexible part of it. When they were done weighing the mother and checking her teeth, they got to work on the cubs. As they tagged the ear of the first cub, its scream rent the air. He knew the acoustics inside the space made it sound worse than it was, but he cringed. "Is he hurt?"

Cate made eye contact. "Just a little pinch, like a human getting their ear pierced. He'll be fine."

Cate looked at a young man with glasses. "Do you have the Vicks, Joey?"

Joey pulled out a jar of Vicks Vapor Rub and handed it to her.

Malachi quirked an eyebrow.

"We'll cover the cubs with it," Cate said.

"It keeps her from smelling the other sow?" Malachi cocked his head.

"Yes. We cover her cubs and the newly introduced one with it.

She'll lick it off of them, replacing it with her own scent. Then it's far more likely she'll accept the orphaned cub." Cate smiled.

"Cool."

She finished up her work and handed him one of the cubs. They moved quickly to cover the cubs with a thin layer of vapor rub. The distinct menthol odor filled his nostrils. Then all three cubs were placed up against the sow where they quickly got back to suckling. The cubs had only spent one night at his place before being taken to the wildlife rehab center, but knowing he wouldn't likely ever see the little fuzz balls again was bittersweet. They were getting the care they needed and each one would be placed in a den with a loving mama bear, but he'd never again get to feed them their bottles.

"Won't the medication you gave the sow to knock her out hurt the cubs?"

"It's a short-acting tranquilizer. She'll be coming out of it any minute now, which means we need to skedaddle."

They quickly packed up their things and headed back the way they'd come. Cate walked beside him, and he slowed his pace to get a moment alone with her.

"Thanks for inviting me to come along."

"You're welcome." The light in her eyes attested to the truth of her words. "I'm glad you came. You'll see what, if anything, happens to the poacher who killed our orphans' mother, but I guess you don't get to see this side of things as often."

"You're right, I don't. From time to time I get to be there for a release, but this case was my first bear-cub encounter in the wild." He had the ridiculous urge to push the hair that had fallen out of her braid back behind her ear, but he fought it. Yes, they'd formed something of a friendship, but a move like that would be far too intimate. "I'll tell you what, I'll call you if we arrest the poacher. You deserve to see justice done, too."

She tilted her head to the side and twirled one of her braids around her index finger. "You would do that for me?"

"Most certainly." He grinned. And it would give him an excuse to call.

"I'm glad we were on it together."

Jack turned around. "Cate, you have a second?"

"Guess I better see what he needs."

Malachi nodded. He hated to see her go, but she had a job to do.

Joey, the college-aged kid on Cate's team, pushed his dark-brown glasses up on his nose with his index finger. "I heard this place was more than a munitions factory. Some say radioactive material from the Manhattan Project was stored here."

"You don't say?" Malachi said. He'd read as much on the internet, but didn't know how much of what he read was fact and how much was fiction. What he did know was that he had a case file sitting on his desk, and the longer he spent out here, the colder it would get.

BECKY PERCHED ON A tree stump and fiddled with a pine cone while the men set up camp. The site was close enough to the park where Malachi worked that she might occasionally catch a glimpse of him, but if she was going to gain her rightful position, she needed him to rejoin the community. Convincing him to do so might prove challenging. He didn't trust her, and once he learned she was his mother, he'd trust her even less. As much as she wanted to get to know him as a person, that couldn't be her top concern. She needed him here. Once he was back home, they could take their time getting reacquainted.

She took a deep breath of cool air laced with the scent of earth and pine.

If she'd known she wouldn't be able to have any more children, she would've taken him with her. Time had proved her unable to conceive, and thus useless for the purpose of procreation, she'd been given other tasks. They'd treated her like a grandmother before she was thirty. Here she was, forty-six years old. If she didn't find a way to change things, she'd wind up a lonely old lady living in a homeless shelter. The community didn't have members over fifty. In her early years, it hadn't occurred to her that it was odd. Now she grew closer to that magic number. What had become of those who aged out? Was that even a thing? Or did they leave on their own? There was no doubt in her mind what happened to those who chose to leave. She'd seen firsthand what Reece did to defectors. Shutting her eyes against the vision of the execution-style killing, she rubbed her thumb and forefinger over her furrowed brow. The last thing she needed was to develop more wrinkles.

Soft footfalls sounded behind her. She turned to see Dorcas.

"Reece would like to speak with you. He's over by the van."

Becky stood. Time to face the consequences of sharing with Malachi what she knew about the cubs. She chewed on her bottom lip as she trudged over rocks and tree roots.

Reece leaned against the driver's door, his arms crossed over his chest. She stopped a few feet before him. "You wanted to see me."

"We have a rat." She swallowed the lump in her throat and forced her breathing to remain calm. "We do?"

"Someone let the authorities know about a trade we were

making. The last thing we need is people nosing around our business." His pale-blue eyes pierced hers. "What I need from you is your listening skills."

Her heartbeat steadied. He wasn't confronting her. What he wanted was her help. This was perfect. "Okay."

"You're practically invisible around here. A fixture. You can listen to conversations without being noticed."

The truth of his words slammed into her, but she rubbed her hands on her skirt and remained quiet.

"Do what you do best. Listen to conversations. Find out if someone here is plotting to bring me down."

She nodded, unsure if this was a trap. Even if it was, she couldn't give herself away. Her best bet was to agree for now and figure it out later. "All right. I can do that."

"Report only to me."

"Of course." As she walked away, she sighed. Asked to investigate her own crime. Now she could pin it on whomever she wanted. What she truly wanted was to get Dorcas out of the way, but she'd settle for setting up Byron. Eunice would fall with him. Then plans could be made for destroying Dorcas. One enemy at a time, she'd watch them all fall. A frisson of discomfort floated through her stomach, but she reminded herself that it was them or her.

Chapter Fifteen

Malachi shoved the slip of paper with Ezekiel James' phone number on it into his pocket as he ascended the steps to his parents' house. His real parents. The ones who had taken him in when nobody else wanted him. The people who had made sure he got a college degree. He wouldn't be calling the man who gave him life. Not now. Not ever.

His father came to the door, a wide smile on his face. "This is a pleasant surprise. Thought you said you couldn't make it to Sunday dinner."

"My plans changed, so here I am. Hope Mom doesn't mind the extra person."

Dad held the door wide and Malachi stepped inside and joined the others around the dining room table. His foster siblings ranged in age from seventeen to thirty-seven. And every single one of them knew God had blessed them when he'd placed them with the Lubach family. After a few minutes of catching up, Mom came in with the first of the dishes. "Help me set this food out on the table, would ya, hon." She smiled in his direction, and he hurried into the kitchen to help. "Are you dating anyone?"

He chuckled. "I haven't settled down with a nice young woman since you asked me a week ago."

"What about that dinner date you had?"

"I had a meal with a colleague. It wasn't a date."

"Keep telling yourself that if you like." She lifted the green bean casserole and pointed to the sweet potatoes. "You get that one. Maybe you should ring her. Women like it when a guy they like calls."

"And what excuse would I have to call her?"

"Tell her you wanted to hear her voice. She'll melt."

"Ma, you're trouble." After setting down the dish, he kissed her on the cheek then took his spot at the table. He should've known she didn't need help, just wanted to meddle in his love life. A flash of Jill brought a smile to his lips. Yes, she'd been meddling for a long time. His first love moving to Hawaii had wounded his mom more than it had him. Which proved they weren't meant to be.

Maybe he should give Cate a ring. She was on his mind far more than was normal for someone he barely knew. More than Jill ever had been. And he wouldn't mind hearing her voice, his foster mother was right about that. He pictured her as she'd been the morning they'd hiked to the bear den together. The vulnerability she'd shown when she'd had the asthma attack, combined with her strength of spirit and determination to find the person responsible for harming the bears drew him to her.

They were kindred spirits. Both fighting for vulnerable creatures who needed their protection.

Keisha elbowed him. "You got a girlfriend?"

"No. I do not have a girlfriend."

Taylor grinned. "Nobody believes you. Definitely sounds like there's a girl."

He laughed at his brother.

"What's her name?" Keisha asked.

He shook his head.

"Might as well tell us." Ben sat seconds before their father took his seat at the head of the table and they all joined hands as he asked the blessing on the meal. Saved by the prayer.

Malachi filled his plate and listened to the conversations buzzing around the table. He didn't need his birth family. His blessings were all about him. They were abundant, and they were real. Seeing Becky had messed with his head, making him want answers to questions that didn't matter. Why did she leave him behind? Why didn't she love him enough to stay? But none of that mattered. God had a plan, and it all worked out for the best. Yet, whenever his thoughts wandered back to that day at the shelter when he'd realized she was gone, he couldn't prevent the squeezing in his heart. She'd broken his eight-year-old heart, and even now at thirty-two, he couldn't revisit the memory without reliving that pain.

Becky watched as Reece went inside his cabin alone. She knew he liked to rest around this time every day. It was hit or miss whether he would fall asleep or not. Dorcas and Eunice were at the stream doing laundry, so this was Becky's chance. If she could grab his cell phone, she might be able to do a little unauthorized snooping.

The kind that would help her and Malachi. Maybe even Clarence, but before she could commit to him, she had to find out if there was any chance for her and Zeke. Which meant finding Ezekiel and asking him if he intended to return to Jade.

The door to the camper creaked as she pushed it open. The overpowering aroma of diapers left in a garbage can too long greeted her, and dust motes floated in the late afternoon sun. She'd nearly made it to the table where his cell phone sat when his voice stopped her dead in her tracks.

He was lying on the couch facing the door. "You have new information for me?"

Forcing down the bile forming in the back of her throat, Becky blinked repeatedly.

"Did you hear my question, woman?"

She closed her eyes and turned to face him, trying to keep her features as neutral as possible. "Sorry. Yeah. I heard some things."

"Well, don't keep me in suspense. Spill it."

"You won't like it."

He rose to his feet, taking up too much space in the trailer. "Tell me."

" have been talking about how if something happens to you, Byron will be in charge and Walter can be second in command." It was true enough. Might not be a word-for-word replay, but they did have a casual conversation about what would happen when and if Reece disappeared. It hadn't been the menacing type, but no reason he needed to know that part.

"Where'd you hear that?"

"Overheard them when they were chopping wood."

"Keep your ears open. I want to know everything that goes on around here."

"All right."

"You keep doing what I ask of you, and you'll be fine. Understand?"

She swallowed hard. "Yes." If she got her way, she'd be out of here soon and would be forced to do Reece's bidding no longer.

"Go on. Get out of here."

CATE STARTED TO SIT in her favorite spot on the sofa, but Penny beat her to it. She scooped up the cat and placed her in her lap. "You can't have my spot, Penny girl." A soft purring answered her, and she leaned her head back on the sofa and inhaled the soft scent of peppermint and chamomile her aromatherapy diffuser emitted.

A ringing came from her cell. Malachi. Probably work-related. She reminded herself that she was in control. Another ring. She could answer it or let it go to voicemail. It was entirely her decision. Another deep breath. A fourth ring. Her desire to talk to him overcame her wish to avoid the telephone. She answered. "Hello."

"Cate. It's Malachi."

She smiled. "I know. Your number is programmed."

"I'm not sure why I'm calling."

She almost wished it was a video call, so she could read his expressions. "You're not?"

"My mom told me to tell you I just wanted to hear your voice.

, it's true. I did want to hear your voice."

"You did?"

"Corny. I know. Sorry. I'm rambling."

His stammering was endearing. And she didn't need him to be so sweet. He was cute enough without the added adorableness. Maybe phone calls with him weren't so bad. "You're not rambling. And I believe I would like your mom."

"You would. She's the best."

She could picture his smile and it made her wish he was closer, so they could meet somewhere. "My brothers looked you up."

"Why would they do that?"

She laughed. "Because they're insane. And they didn't believe me when I told them we were just colleagues."

"Are we? Just colleagues, I mean."

Her heart beat faster as she considered his question. She wouldn't mind being more than that, but how would they make it work? "I don't know. Anything more will be difficult with us living so far apart." But that didn't stop her from wanting to go out with him.

"True. I keep telling myself the same thing." He sighed. "But if we don't make an effort to see each other again, there is a good chance we won't. I don't want to lose touch."

"Me neither."

"I'd like to get to know you better. Would you be open to me taking you out when we both have a day off?"

Usually when guys wanted to get to know her better, it was because they'd found out about her father. Somehow, she didn't think that was the case this time. "I can make my own schedule, so why don't you let me know when you're available, and I'll take the day off."

"How's Thursday?"

He wasn't wasting any time, was he? Probably a good thing. It wouldn't give her time to freak out and change her mind. "Perfect." She rattled off her address. "I'm in the apartment over the garage."

"I'll text you the details tomorrow. Once I figure out what we should do with our day."

"Sounds good. We're going to place Bitsy in a den in the Poconos on Wednesday, so I'll be able to let you know how things go."

"Bitsy?" He chuckled. "I didn't know you named them. It's cute."

"That's what I call her in my head, but I didn't mean to say it out loud."

"It's okay to give them names. Don't believe that nonsense about imprinting on them by giving them names. If anyone caused them harm, it was the wildlife traffickers who were trying to sell them to the highest bidder. I'm glad you found her a home. If you don't want to rush back in time for Thursday, we could go out next week."

"I'd be coming home either way. I only stayed in town when I was working at Worlds End because it was an excuse to visit my brother." She'd might've stayed longer than initially planned because of Malachi, but he didn't need to know that. "I'm looking forward to Thursday."

"Me too."

"Okay." Malachi wanted to see her again. She had the strangest urge to do a happy dance. And she might've done just that if she hadn't been afraid she'd disturb Penny.

Chapter Sixteen

Cate and her team had spent all day Wednesday at Big Pocono State Park. The park wouldn't reopen for the season until April, which made it easier to do their job, but now that they were done, she dreaded the nearly three-hour drive home. Malachi had been right when he suggested postponing. She'd told a little white lie when she said she would've gone home anyway. If she hadn't wanted to get home to see him, she would've stayed in a hotel overnight. Truth was she wanted to see him and had let that desire win out over her own common sense. Nevertheless, when his text message came through, she couldn't keep the skip out of her step when she saw his name come across the screen. She got in the car and tapped the text to read it.

Malachi: Can you be ready by 7:30?

Cate: Sure thing. Are we getting dinner, or should I eat first?

Malachi: 7:30 a.m.

Cate: Oh. Okay. I'll be ready.

Malachi: I'll bring coffee and scones.

She could get used to a man who brought her coffee and scones.

Cate: Sounds good. See you tomorrow.

As she tucked her phone back into the console and started her truck, it rang. Seeing his name there she answered. "Hi there."

"Texting is okay, but I'd rather hear your voice."

"I'm glad you called." For some reason, talking to him on the phone didn't raise her anxiety levels the same way they did when she spoke to most people. In fact, she found herself grinning like a fool. "Out of curiosity, where on earth are we going at 7:30 in the morning?"

"The only thing I could find to do that early. A bird walk at the arboretum."

"That sounds like fun."

"I thought you'd like it. Figured the earlier we started our day, the more time we could spend together before I had to have you home."

"That sounds nice. I'm looking forward to tomorrow."

"Me too. How did today go? Did Bitsy take well to her new home?"

Cate pictured the cub as she'd left her suckling from her adoptive mother. "It went well."

"That's good. I'll let you go. I know you're ."

"We finished a little early, so I'm getting ready to head back now."

"That's great. Make sure you get a good night's sleep."

"I'll try." She probably wouldn't get much sleep. This was her first date in a long time. Since she left University of Pennsylvania in favor of the wildlife biology program at Penn State. A choice her father still lamented, but it was hers to make and now that she was in the field, she was glad she'd chosen the career path she had. It was perfect for her. "See you in the morning." Her smile lingered as she headed down the mountain. He was the first man who'd ever called so he could hear her voice. Yeah. She might just be smitten.

MALACHI PULLED UP OUTSIDE of the house where Cate rented an apartment. They had a busy day ahead of them. They would end their date with a Zach Bryan concert over at the Bryce Jordan Center, but he hadn't told her that part yet. He wasn't into country music himself, but he'd caught it coming from the speakers in her car more than once, so he was taking the chance that she was a fan and would appreciate going to the concert.

He hurried up the stairs leading to the apartment over the garage. His mind wasn't on the day ahead of them though. Kevin called while he was making the scones to let him know that from what he'd discovered it looked like the community Ezekiel James had started had been reformed and was thriving.

The last he could find, they'd been chased off their land.

That might explain why his mother was in Pennsylvania. He wondered if she'd returned to West Virginia yet. He had so many questions for her, but, at present, he had no clue how to find her. Cate answered his knock and ushered him inside. Her calico cat perched herself on the top of the sofa and watched as Cate slipped on her shoes and grabbed her backpack purse.

Once inside the car, her eyes widened. "I smell them. Where did you hide them?"

He laughed, and the release was nice. Reaching into the backseat, he snagged the paper lunch sack and handed it to her. "Your coffee is in the cup holder."

"I don't know how you managed to avoid the altar. You cook. You make coffee. You, sir, are a catch."

"Let's see if you still think that by the end of our date."

Her grin lit up her entire face. He could get used to seeing her smile. Hopefully, she'd enjoy the day, and he'd have more chances to spend time with her in the future.

In a clearing in the woods, Becky stood beside Reece. He'd forced her to join him even when she'd tried to make excuses why she couldn't. Bile rose in her throat as Byron and Walter were forced to their knees. This was her fault. She could speak now and save them, but then the bullet would penetrate the back of *her* skull instead. She closed her eyes.

Reece's arm circled her neck. "I want you to watch. You provided the intel that will end their lives. It seems fitting you should watch their executions. He was toying with her. She was almost certain he knew she'd lied, but doubt niggled around the edges of her consciousness as Reece released her and fired his weapon. Two shots in quick succession. No room for error. It was over, but her body shook uncontrollably.

"Don't worry, Becky. They won't be causing any more trouble for us. Now you can resume your normal duties without fear of them usurping my authority."

He wasn't the authority. The jade was, and she'd kept it hidden all these years. Now Malachi had it, and once the rest of the community knew it, he would be their true leader. He'd be able to communicate with the gods through the jade. All she needed to do was release her doubts and trust the jade. Just because she hadn't been able to use it the way Ezekiel had didn't make it any less real. It obviously didn't communicate with women. Why that surprised her, she couldn't say. She'd accepted that she wouldn't be the leader, but someone had to remove Reece from that position.

Cate's throat was raw from singing along during the concert. Malachi reached for her hand, and she could think of no good reason not to thread her fingers with his. He was incredible. A morning bird walk. Lunch at Allen Street Grill. Then a concert. It was an incredible day. Exhausting, but wonderful. He released her hand and opened the passenger door for her and she slid into his truck for the drive back to her apartment. They pulled up outside her place but remained in the vehicle, both silent for a long moment.

"I'd welcome you in, but it's late."

"Let me walk you to your door."

She nodded, and he slipped out and came around to her side, offering his hand as she stepped down. When they reached her door, she unlocked it, then turned to face him. His eyes met hers, and she could see the question there.

"I'd better get inside."

"Good night, Cate." His lips brushed hers before he lifted her chin so she was forced to meet his eyes. "I'd like to do this again. Soon."

"The kiss?" It may have been quick, but even after he'd pulled away, she could feel where his lips had touched hers. A repeat performance would be welcome.

"Yes, but I meant the date. Will you go out with me again?"

"I'd love to."

His lips met hers in another gentle kiss. Just a whisper of his lips against hers. It wasn't enough. She wanted more. Her arms circled his neck, and her fingers got lost in his soft waves. A moan escaped her throat, reminding her that a kiss was as far as it could go.

A throat cleared behind her, and she jumped.

"What have we here?" Grayson asked.

Heat rushed to her face. Only her brother would show up when they knew she was out on a date. She had the most embarrassing family in the universe. "What are you doing in my apartment?" Her tone came out exasperated, but she didn't care. He shouldn't be here.

The murderous expression in Malachi's eyes made her shake her head and place a calming hand on his bicep. "It's just my brother."

Gray moved out of the way so she could enter. He leaned against the wall, crossing his feet at the ankles. "Maggie gave me a key, so I could wait up here and make sure you got home all right."

Cate gestured for Malachi to join them inside. "I guess you'd better come in. If you don't, my brother will follow you home and interrogate you there."

"You half expected him to be here, didn't you?" Malachi asked.

"I'd be lying if I said no." She let out a strangled laugh. "I looked for his Bronco when we rode down the street, but I didn't see it."

"I brought the Lexus. Figured it would blend better."

"Boundaries. Ever heard of them?" she asked.

He stuck his hand out to Malachi. She shook her head. "Don't shake his hand."

But she was too late, Malachi was already wincing. "Firm handshake you've got there."

"What are your intentions with my sister?" Gray asked as he flopped down on her sofa.

Cate rolled her eyes.

"You do know that this was our first date, right?"

"Now that he stuck his tongue down your throat, you'll admit to dating him, sis?"

"It was a tame kiss by anyone's standards. There is something seriously wrong with you, Gray." She gestured to the arm chair and waited until Malachi sat, then settled on the sofa beside Grayson. "He asked me out. I said yes. We had a delightful day. Until you showed up."

"Good thing I did, too."

"And why is that?"

"To keep things from going too far."

"I'm a grown woman. He's a grown man."

"You're a Christian girl. Raised in a faith-filled home."

"Can I say something?" Malachi raised his hand. At Gray's nod, he continued. "We had already said good night when you cleared your throat."

"I know my own mind, and I don't need you to fight my battles." Cate forced herself to keep her volume and tone steady. She loved Grayson, but enough was enough.

"I can think of a time or two when having me and Gavin around was beneficial."

She crossed her arms over her chest. "Samantha was the real life saver."

"No doubt about it. She rescued us all on Red Rock Mountain." Gray rubbed the back of his neck and gave her a hard smile. "But tonight, she's not here. I am."

"Fine. You win. Have fun interrogating Malachi. I'll make tea."

She sent her date a look that she hoped conveyed an apology. "Best to get this over with if you're serious about a second date. Peace won't be had until Gray gives his approval. Even then, I'm sure you'll need to pass Gavin's tests, too."

Once she set the water on to boil, she fell into a chair and placed her forehead on the table. If Malachi had any desire to see her again after tonight, it'd be a miracle, but it also might prove that he was a man worth taking a chance on. Maybe Grayson's arrival would prove providential. A means for testing the strength of the tenuous bond that was forming between them. Prayer didn't come as easy as it once had, but she lifted up a prayer for Malachi. He'd need it.

Chapter Seventeen

On the way to work the following morning, Malachi ruminated on his introduction to Cate's eldest brother the night before. From what she'd told him, he'd expected overprotective brothers, but Grayson was a touch extreme. There had been hints of a story behind his need to guard her. He'd sensed a past trauma in their unspoken signals and even a few of the things they spoke aloud. Would she feel comfortable enough to tell him her story anytime soon? He'd opened up to her, but she hadn't reciprocated.

There was a folder on his desk when he arrived at the office. Kevin must've left it there. He rifled through it and sat up straighter, forcing himself to slow down and read every word. When he finished going through the paperwork, he rubbed his eyes. After a sleepless night, the last thing he needed was a stressful day at work, but it looked like the kid managed to get his hands on FBI and West Virginia State Police reports. On short notice. He couldn't help but admire the younger man's diligence.

If what he was looking at proved true, and it seemed likely that would be the case, his mother's community was involved in wildlife trafficking down in their home state before moving their operation north. But it was their other occupation that made him do a double-take. They'd long been suspected of arms trafficking, and their new leader Reece Mclean was believed to be Maurice Moretti, a contract killer who'd worked up and down the east coast. When things heated up too much, he must've found refuge in the relative anonymity of the cult.

He flashed back to Becky sitting in his office, her hands trembling and her eyes widening as she asked him if he'd be able to arrest Reece. If he'd known more about the man at the time, he would've had him in cuffs and he would've called down the FBI to see if they wanted him. If not, he'd have handed him off to West Virginia, but he'd let him slip right through his fingers.

"You all right?" Kevin stopped at his desk.

He raked a hand through his hair. "I'm not thrilled that I let this guy get away."

Kevin straightened his glasses. "You couldn't have known."

"I don't know about that. If I'd enlisted your help sooner, we might've known before they split."

"You're kind of a lone wolf sometimes, but don't beat yourself up. You did your best."

"No, I didn't, but thanks for your hard work. How late did you stay here digging into this?"

"A couple of hours." Kevin gave him a pointed look. "I could show you how I do it, but then you wouldn't need me."

"Not true." This wasn't the first time he'd realized too late that he should've relied more on Kevin. His fellow park ranger might be younger, but he had skills Malachi lacked. They would complement each other if he allowed the younger ranger's assistance more often. But right now, he needed to focus on the present problem. "How would you feel about taking care of Titan and Pixie while I take a little trip?"

Kevin shrugged. "Sure thing. I've got your back. Do what you need to do."

West Virginia. He would follow the instructions in his mother's message and uncover the roots of his past. Going back was the only way forward. He needed to find out how the Jade community wound up under the leadership of a killer. And in order to figure out where they were now, he needed to figure out where they'd been and had to try to put himself in the mind of a murderer.

Cate stared at Malachi's contact information on her cell phone. She'd been wrestling with herself for ten minutes about whether or not to call him. No man in his right mind would want to see her again after being forced to endure Grayson's questions. He'd been in good humor when he left. Had even gotten Gray to laugh when the conversation turned away from her and toward spring training. She was glad they could talk baseball. It wasn't a subject that interested her in the slightest, but if it gave them a safe topic to discuss, she was all for it.

She sucked in a breath for courage and hit the call button.

Malachi picked up on the first ring. "Hi, Cate."

"Hi." She looked out her bedroom window and focused her

attention on the tree line. The trees were starting to bud. Spring was around the corner. "I'm sorry about Gray."

"Unless you called him and set the whole thing up, there is nothing to apologize for. He's a grown man and made his own decision to show up at your place."

"Nonetheless, I know it was awkward and weird."

"It was."

She blinked back tears. This was it. Where he would tell her that he couldn't deal with her family. It happened every time she met someone she thought was a decent guy.

"Your brothers aren't going to scare me away that easily. I have to take a trip to West Virginia, but when I return, I'd love to take you out again. If you're game?"

Her eyes closed, and she sent up a silent prayer of thanksgiving. "I'd like that. Why are you going to West Virginia?"

"Let's make a deal. I'll tell you all about my trip after you tell me a few things about yourself. You've been holding back, and if we're going to get to know each other, it's a two-way street."

"What if I came with you?" The words came out before she had time to think them through. She had a job to do. Taking time off without any notice was crazy. Yet, if she was going to take a chance on this man, what better way to do it than to spend a few days together.

"I don't plan overnights with a woman I just started dating."

"I wasn't suggesting we stay in the same room."

"Are you serious? You would drop everything and join me?"

"Yes. I'll get my own room, obviously, but it'll be a chance for us to spend time together."

"Leave the booking to me," he said.

"I promise not to tell my brothers where I am." She wouldn't mention that Grayson lived and worked in Virginia. That fact would not help her case.

"I wouldn't put it past Grayson to show up."

"You know what? Forget it. I don't know what I was thinking inviting myself to join you. I'm sorry. We'll talk when you come home."

"I'd love for you to join me. I leave in the morning. Can you get away with so little notice?"

"I'll call my boss and find out." She pinched the bridge of her nose. "Are you sure I'm not intruding?"

"There is nobody I'd rather have beside me on this trip, but you'd better be prepared to open up, because I'm going to have no choice but to tell you all about my own issues if you're tagging along."

Was she ready to share her past with him? She swallowed the lump in her throat. It wasn't something that came up often. Most people would talk about themselves for hours. Nobody asked about her unless they made the connection to her father, then the questions never stopped coming. He didn't yet know she was the daughter of the billionaire CEO of Garrison Industries, Grayson Garrison, Sr. She would've thought after being introduced to her brother, he would've put it together, but as far as she could tell, he hadn't yet connected those dots. But now she'd have to tell him or risk losing the chance at something that might turn out to be great.

"You still there, Cate?"

"I am."

"Text me after you talk to your boss. If it's a go, I'll send you the flight details."

She wasn't sure she'd ever taken a commercial flight. No doubt she could use the private jet, but then she wouldn't have a chance to explain things to Malachi beforehand. And using it would tell her brothers exactly where she'd gone. They'd find her anyway if they were so inclined, but no need to make it easy for them. "Okay."

Chapter Eighteen

Becky peered in the window of Reece's camper. He'd sent Dorcas and the kids out and the last she'd seen them they were heading down a trail that led to an old fire tower. The sun was warm, the temperature in the sixties or so, so at least he hadn't put his family out in the cold this time. His cell phone was beside the sink, and he was dozing in bed. If she didn't find a way to get online and search for Ezekiel, all her carefully laid plans would be for naught. She had to find out whether Zeke or Malachi was their next true leader. It had to be one of them. And if it was Zeke, he would need to get the jade from Malachi.

This was her chance, but if she messed up again, he'd know that her coming in while he was sleeping was a conscious choice not an accident. If he figured that out, she was as good as dead.

After kicking her shoes off at the door, she slipped into the camper in her stocking feet and carefully tiptoed. Her arm brushed against a pitcher, causing it to teeter on the edge of the counter. Her heartbeat was deafening as she steadied it before it could crash to the ground. A quick sweep of the space assured her that Reece remained asleep. She snatched up the cell phone and stuffed it in the pocket of her skirt before picking her way back out. As she stepped through the door, she came face to face with Eunice.

"What were you doing in there?"

Becky held a finger up to her lips. "Reece has me working on something, and I came by to give him a report, but he was sleeping, so I'll come back later."

"Everyone knows he lays down around this time."

"It's not like I have a clock. Didn't realize it had gotten so late."

Eunice smiled. "You're up to something. I can tell, but I'm not planning to say anything. Reece scares me. Whatever you're up to, I'm sure it's better than our current situation."

"If you hate it here, why stay?"

"Everybody knows that nobody can leave."

Becky nodded. "There's only one way out."

"Good luck." Eunice gave her a half smile. "Do yourself a favor and don't trust Dorcas. She loves him."

"I know she does." And it saddened her. Reece was worthless, but the girl had great potential. He needed to go, and as much as Dorcas got under Becky's skin, she hated to see her suffer the way she had when she was in her position and had it all stolen from her the night they'd thrown Ezekiel into prison.

CATE SHOWERED AND DRESSED. In his text last night, Malachi asked if she minded if they drive instead of fly. Truth be told, she preferred driving. Flying twisted her stomach into knots.

Staring at herself in the floor-length mirror, she frowned. She wanted to be comfortable for the five-hour drive, but she also wanted to look cute. Jeans and a baby-doll style shirt hugged her figure, but not in a 'look at me' way. The outfit was conservative by today's standards. Of course, her brothers would probably think she'd dressed too sexy if she wore a potato sack. There was no pleasing them.

Instead of her usual signature pigtails, she'd left her hair down. It fell in soft waves over her shoulders. A mistake? She still had time to secure it in braids before he arrived. A soft knock sounded on the door. Or not. He was early.

After checking to make sure it was Malachi, she opened the door for him. "Come on in. I just need to grab my overnight bag."

She went into her room and snatched up her black-and-white-patterned Vera Bradley bag. A gift from Brittany before her abduction. Her friend hadn't been the same since her trauma. Cate straightened her shoulders, took a deep breath, and headed back out to the front room.

When she dropped the bag by the door, Malachi rose from where he'd been sitting on the couch and joined her. He took both of her hands in his. "You look amazing."

Warmth flooded her face, and she prayed she wasn't turning bright red. "Thanks."

"And the blush makes you even more attractive."

"You're out of your mind, mister."

He dropped her hands and brought his right hand up to cup her face. His touch set the butterflies to dancing in her stomach, and when he released her and brushed his knuckles against her neck her knees went weak. "You smell great, too. What is that, apples?"

"It's my perfume. I think there is a hint of some kind of fruit in the fragrance, but I'm no expert."

"I'm going with pear and maybe grapefruit. Whatever it is it's working for you."

"I'm glad you like it." She didn't often wear fragrance since she spent most of her time in the woods and didn't want the wildlife to smell her coming, but this morning she'd dabbed a little on her wrists and the hollow of her throat at the last minute. A good decision, clearly.

"This is the first time I've seen you without the braids. You're cute with them, but you're stunning with your hair down." His thumb brushed along her jawline, touching the sensitive skin under her ear. When his eyes moved to her lips, she held her breath, but abruptly he stepped back without the expected kiss. "You ready to go?"

She nodded.

He picked up her bag and turned to go. Why hadn't he kissed her? Tears stung the backs of her eyes, but she blinked them away. It wasn't a rejection. Maybe he was afraid of where it would lead if he kissed her again while they were alone in her apartment. They were both Christians, and he seemed to take his faith seriously. He shouldn't have worried about it though, she wouldn't have let anything happen. Yes. That had to be it. If it was anything more than that, he wouldn't have driven all the way out to State College to pick her up, right?

Malachi merged onto the highway and turned the radio down a few notches to allow it to provide background noise without interrupting their conversation. "You're quiet."

"So are you."

As he drove, he made small talk about the weather, his favorite hiking trails, and other inconsequential things.

As much as he preferred to keep his investigation to himself, he was willing to tell Cate about it. But he'd been vulnerable with her more than once. And listening to her and Grayson talk had made one thing clear. There was a reason her brothers were the way they were, and he wanted to know what it was. He didn't know much about her beyond her love for animals and her incredible personality. If they were going to explore a relationship, he needed to know more about her. He didn't want to push her too far and scare her away, but when she remained quiet two hours into the drive, he sighed. "We made a deal, Cate. It's time to tell me something about yourself."

"What do you want to know about me?"

"For starters, you could tell me about your mother. I get the feeling she isn't in the picture."

"My mom died."

Getting her to share shouldn't be this hard. He'd given her so many openings not only on this drive, but when they'd been out on their date last Thursday. "How did she die?"

"Breast cancer."

Man, that was a tough break. No wonder she didn't want to talk about it. "How old were you?"

"Thirteen."

"I've never been a young girl, but I've heard that's a rough age without the trauma of losing your mother. I can't imagine what that must've been like."

"It wasn't ideal." She rested her head against the seat and stared up at the ceiling of the car. "Are you sure you want to hear this?"

"There isn't much in this life that I'm sure about, but I do want to get to know you better, and in the time we've spent together, you haven't been forthcoming."

"That's likely because when guys learn more about me, it isn't me that piques their interest."

"Now *that's* a statement that needs an explanation."

"My father is a wealthy businessman." She sighed. "When a guy I'm dating figures out who my dad is, his interest in me increases, but so do the questions about my father and how much of his money is in trust for me, and how much will I inherit if he dies. You know the drill."

"Can't say that I do, but I can assure you that I'm not interested in you for your father's money."

"How can you know that? You don't even know who he is."

"After that interrogation from Grayson, you don't think I looked him up? Found out that he's a billionaire mogul's son? Putting two and two together wasn't that hard."

"So, you knew?"

"I still wanted to hear about it from you. I also saw an article about the Continental Alliance. Your name was in the headline, but I didn't read it. Something told me that was a story you needed to tell me yourself."

"Not while we're driving. I don't drink, but telling that story would be easier after a few shots."

"Yes, I imagine that's true, but would you be willing to settle for a cup of hot chocolate? I packed some packets in my bag. Something told me we'd need them."

"Yes. I think I can open up to you as we sip cocoa. If there is a fire in the hearth, it'll be even easier."

"That can be arranged. I rented an Airbnb. It has separate bedrooms as requested. The view is fabulous, and there is a huge fireplace in the front room."

She reached across the console and squeezed his knee. Thankfully, her hand returned to her lap. Otherwise, concentrating on the road would've been impossible.

Chapter Nineteen

"You ever going to tell me what we're doing here?" Cate stared at the dancing flames and gripped her mug with both hands.

"Not until you open up to me."

"I did. You know about my dad and my mom. You met my brother. You saw where I live."

He took the cup from her hands and drew her closer to him on the couch.

"Just the facts. That's your style, and I get it. I'm usually the same way, but I want more from you. Are you willing to share your heart with me, Cate?"

Her pulse sped up. What he was asking was risky. If she trusted him with her deepest secrets, and he walked away, she'd be crushed. And she wasn't sure she could handle that. Life had been harsh enough. "My heart? What do you mean by that?"

"Relationships are built on more than facts. I'm not interested in a casual relationship. If we're going to date, I want to know that there is a chance for a future between us. There isn't if it's going to be one-sided."

"You wanted to know about the article." Her eyes searched his as she made the conscious decision to trust him. "You really didn't read it?"

He shook his head. "Felt something inside telling me not to. Don't know if it was the Holy Spirit or simple intuition, but I chose to wait. I plan to read it, but I'd rather hear it from you first."

Her mind raced. The Holy Spirit. She'd stopped listening years ago. Maybe if she trusted Him, it would be easier to trust Malachi. His motives seemed pure, but it was like taking a plunge off a cliff into ice-cold water. It would be exhilarating, but might also prove a fatal error. Lifting a prayer for it to all turn out all right, she sucked in a breath before starting her story. "A few years ago, a friend of mine disappeared from our campus. At the time, I was attending the University of Pennsylvania."

"Wow. And you switched to Penn State. Why?"

"Let me finish, and you'll hear the whole of it."

He made a zipping motion across his lips and sat back, allowing her to continue her story.

"My roommate, Brittany, wanted to join a sorority. They'd asked me first, and I'd shot them down, but they wouldn't let her join without me, so I agreed. The next thing I know they have us doing some questionable things as pledges, but I ignored all the warning signs because I didn't want to disappoint my friend. I didn't have many of them. Growing up a billionaire's daughter can be isolating. I did have one other friend at the school, Emmaline. She was the daughter of one of my dad's friends. A federal judge. Around the time we joined the sorority, Emmaline went missing. Everyone thought she'd run off with her boyfriend until he showed back up at school without her. That's when things got weird.

"This older man, Mason, tried to get me to go to Emmaline's house and steal something from her father. I suspected something wasn't right, so I contacted another one of my dad's friends who worked for the FBI. He convinced me to go undercover as a guest of the Continental Alliance. The cloak and dagger of it all intrigued me and I agreed to it. There was a problem though. One I didn't find out until much later."

"What was that?"

"The FBI agent I went to was a member of the Continental Alliance, and I wasn't really going undercover, I was a captive."

"Did they hurt you?"

She shook her head. "Thankfully, I was rescued before being 'married off', which was what they called it when they gave a woman to one of their esteemed members, but I'll admit to having trust issues that weren't present before the experience."

Malachi tugged her closer and wrapped her in his arms. "That was so brave of you."

She pulled back and wiped away a tear. "You mean stupid?"

"No. I mean brave."

"If I had been smarter and gone to my father or my brothers instead of going to Dad's friend, my friends might've been spared what they went through there."

"Were they sexually abused?"

Tears streamed down her face, but she didn't answer verbally.

"What happened to them was not your fault. Only those who harmed them are responsible for what occurred."

"Thanks for saying that."

He wiped away her tears. "I'm not just spouting words. They're true. Have you prayed about this? Given it to God?"

She twisted her hands in her lap. "I don't deserve to be free of the guilt, and God is good, so if I ask Him to take it, I know He will."

"Sweetheart, you must ask Him. None of us deserve His gifts, but He gives them to us freely, and I can't imagine living with the weight of my sin. What happened up there wasn't even your fault, so you deserve to be free of it." He pulled her into his chest, and she soaked up his strength as she considered his words.

THE NEXT MORNING AS they dined on biscuits and sausage gravy at the Simply Sweet Cafe, Malachi locked eyes with Cate. She squirmed in her seat before pointing her fork at him. "You never did tell me why we're here."

"I told you about growing up in a cult?"

"You did."

"It was located around here. I need to do the kind of research that can only be done in person by talking to actual people in the area."

"Canvassing, like they do on all the crime television shows?"

He grinned. "Something like that. But our first stop may be a bit unconventional. Get ready to meet my dear old dad."

"Your father led the cult?"

"Yes." He reached across the table for her hands. "He's out of prison and living not too far from here, so I thought I'd start by showing up at his house."

"Unannounced? You're as bad as my brother."

"Best way to catch him off-guard. That's the best way to get suspects to open up. When they're prepared for you, they clam up."

"What exactly is he a suspect in?"

"Well, you know about the poaching and the wildlife trafficking, but what you don't know yet is that the guy we suspected of that is the current leader of my father's cult known as Jade."

"Wow. That's a huge coincidence."

"I don't think it is. I believe my mother somehow must've orchestrated their arrival at Worlds End."

"Are you serious?"

"Yes. Remember I told you about the woman who came in to tell me about the bear cubs?"

"I do."

"She's my biological mother."

"Why didn't you mention that when we were doing surveillance?"

"At the time, I wasn't certain. I suspected, but felt foolish saying it out loud."

"When did you discover the truth?"

"The day I searched the cabin."

"It's strange it hasn't come up since then. You wanted me to open up to you, but you've kept this quiet."

"Well, I didn't want to ruin our date with this kind of talk and the day we placed the cubs there were too many people around."

She stared at him through narrowed eyes. "Likely excuse."

"Now you have the whole story."

"Except how it connects to your biological father and West Virginia."

"Ezekiel James was recently released from prison. He's here, and this is where Jade started. They only recently made the trek to Pennsylvania. I'm not sure if they're back here or not, but I want to find out."

"Isn't this a lot of work for a wildlife trafficking case?"

"It is, but the guy we suspected of that is also wanted by the FBI. They believe that Reece Mclean is actually the notorious Maurice Moretti. When he came to Worlds End, I knew he looked familiar, but I couldn't place him. Maybe his fake West Virginia accent threw me off."

"Ah. And what is he wanted for?"

"You mean you don't know?" He frowned. "Seriously? You've never heard of him?"

"I don't think so."

"He's a mafia hit man."

"Oh. That Maurice Moretti. Yes. The name is familiar. Between the news and a friend's research."

"You had a friend who looked into him?"

"It was a school thing."

"Well, when they finally had a case where they could convict him of his crimes, he disappeared. Apparently to start a new life with the Jade community of believers."

"I heard about him disappearing, but never imagined he'd be connected to our wildlife trafficking case." She sucked in a breath and pushed away her plate. "Okay. Let's do this."

"Not so fast. I'm finishing my breakfast first."

Twenty minutes later, he was ringing the bell at the rundown house listed as his father's residence. When the door opened, Malachi took a step back. Not the man from his memories. He wasn't sure what he'd expected, but the picture he had in his head didn't match the man who had aged twenty-four years in the time they'd been apart. He'd done the math and knew his biological father was sixty-five, but the man standing before him now looked much older. Prison hadn't been easy on him. "Can I help you?"

"Ezekiel James?"

"That's me."

"I'm Malachi James."

The man's expression softened. "It's been a long time. I never thought I'd see you again."

"Or any of your other children, I imagine."

"A few of them have been around since I was released. Wanted to give me a piece of their minds for ruining their lives."

"Shouldn't have surprised you."

His forehead furrowed showing the deep lines that had formed there since Malachi had last seen him. "It didn't. Not at all. Come inside. We're letting all the heat out."

Malachi followed him into the kitchen.

"Sit down. I can tell you have something on your mind. It's strange that you showed up today. I received an odd phone call from your mother earlier. I've no idea how she managed to dig up my cell phone number. It's unlisted."

"She called you?"

"She wanted to see me. Claims to still love me. I think I talked her out of coming here. Told her that our relationship wasn't right. She deserved better."

"Well, I'm here about her. She does deserve better. No woman or child should have to go through what you put her through, but I believe she's in danger once again." He needed to redirect this conversation and get the information he came for. "Were you aware that the community was reestablished after you went to prison?"

"Some of the members of my church mentioned it."

"Your church? Is that what we're calling cults these days?"

Ezekiel tugged at the sleeve of his shirt. "I go to a Baptist church in town. I'm not the same man I was back then."

Malachi released a harsh breath. "Forgive me if I find that difficult to believe. Lord help me, but I would have a tough time letting a pedophile into my church whether he was saved or not."

"That's understandable. All I can say is that I'm sorry for the pain I caused."

"If you weren't a pedophile, I wouldn't be alive. Do you know how messed up that is? Can you understand how that makes a person feel? I've spent my whole adult life wishing I hadn't been born because my conception was wrong. And I've lived with the worry that one day I might become you."

"That won't happen."

"How can you know that?"

"My sinful depravity isn't your destiny. You aren't out there leading your own community of faithful followers, are you?"

Malachi coughed. "Of course not."

"I don't expect you to forgive me, son, but God has." Ezekiel pushed away from the table.

"I spent many nights on my knees praying for your soul," Malachi said. Though he doubted the truth of his father's words, he needed answers, so he didn't want to provoke him. Yes, Jesus could save anyone's rotten soul, but it was hard to believe that a man who claimed to have a direct line to God had given up that fantasy and chosen to follow the truth.

"Thank you for those prayers. They worked." He folded his hands on the table before him. "Now if we're done talking about my past sins, let's focus on what you came here for. What can I do for you?"

"I need to know everything you know about what happened with Jade after you went to prison."

"Wish I could tell you more, but I don't know much. I heard it was restarted by some of the women about a year after it was disbanded. From what I understand, it was mostly women and children, but a few of the original men were also there. About five years ago, a new guy showed up. Claimed to be called by God. You know the deal."

"I do." Malachi stood. "We need to talk to people who might know something. Would you mind sharing the names of those people you talked to at church?"

"Not at all. I'll help in any way I can." He wrote down several names then grabbed a spiral-bound directory from his counter and wrote numbers and email addresses next to the names. He pointed to one of the names with his pen. "Charlie's property abuts the piece of land where they had the new community. He said they cleared out recently. Something about the feds coming down on them again."

Malachi took the page he offered and shoved it into his pocket. "Thanks."

Zeke's gaze turned to Cate. "Is this your wife?"

"This is Cate. We're not married." She was far too good for the likes of him, but if she'd have him, he might see about a future with her. It was too soon to be considering wedding bells, but he wouldn't rule them out either.

Chapter Twenty

Malachi held the passenger door for Cate. "You were awfully quiet in there."

She waited for him to be seated before speaking. "It didn't feel like it was my place to say much."

He gave her hand a squeeze.

She closed her eyes briefly before opening them and seeking eye contact. "Did you mean what you said about praying for him to be saved?"

"My foster parents taught me to pray for my enemies, so yeah, I prayed for him. Often."

"I can't imagine what it must be like to think of your own father as the enemy."

"It's strange. He was kind to me when I was young. I have a few scattered memories, and they're all good. I had this giant resentment against the FBI for separating my family until my late teens when I grew up and saw things clearly for the first time." And that's when the fears of becoming him had started. He swallowed back that old thought. He was his own man, and the horrors his father had committed had nothing to do with him. It wasn't in his DNA, it was in his character. "That's when I came to think of my biological father as the enemy."

"My dad is distant sometimes, and even a touch cold, but what you went through with yours ... It's tragic."

"It's my mother who deserves the sympathy. But I'll admit, it's weird to wish something hadn't happened when that something was what led to your existence."

"I'm sorry that you have to live with that knowledge."

"It's all part of who I am. I've come to accept it. For the most part." He gave her a sad smile. "Let's get out of here. We have an investigation to conduct and confronting him was only step one."

"Where to now?"

"Back to the rental house. From there we can make a few phone calls."

CATE WATCHED MALACHI AS he arranged meetings with a couple of guys from the church Ezekiel James attended.

After ending the call, he smiled. "Charlie has time now. Feel like taking a trip up the mountain?"

"Let's do it."

They arrived at Charlie's homestead shortly after three. Cate followed Malachi and wondered again what she was doing here with him. Spending this much time with him would inevitably lead to heartbreak when he decided he wanted someone who could be home every night and not traveling all over the state tracking wildlife.

A man came out of the house as they climbed the front stairs. "Malachi, I presume?"

"Yes. And this is my girlfriend Cate."

The designation surprised her. It seemed early in their relationship to add labels, but from what he'd shown her of himself so far, she sensed he didn't like games and said what he thought. She smiled and shook the man's hand. "Thanks for talking with us."

"Certainly." He held the door open for them to enter and they shuffled inside. They were led into an office that looked to function as a library as well. What showed of the walls was paneled, but they were lined with floor-to-ceiling shelving and packed with books. Except for one wall behind the desk where a massive buck head was mounted. Certainly not the most appealing of decor in her eyes. And none of the titles she saw made her want to open a book, either. Seemed Charlie was a history buff. Enjoyed reliving the civil war.

He took the seat behind his desk and gestured for them to take the two chairs positioned in front of it. "I'll be honest, I didn't have much of a problem with my neighbors. They kept to themselves for the most part. And I heard from some that the new guy didn't allow drugs and believed in protecting children, so I figured at least that was an improvement."

"Where'd you hear that?" Malachi leaned forward in his chair.

Charlie frowned. "I think it was from Hector. He's across the street from here, down about a half mile."

Malachi's focus never wavered from the other man's face.

Cate studied them both. The subtle shift in Charlie's gaze made her think he was lying. She wondered if Malachi thought the same. "Do you think he'd talk to us?"

"Don't see any reason why not."

The men continued their conversation for another fifteen minutes with Malachi only getting bits and pieces of hearsay from him before he stood. Cate pasted on a smile and hoped the next interview would yield better intel.

BECKY'S EYES NEVER LEFT Reece as she returned his cell phone, careful to avoid banging it as it hit the table. She held her breath as she tiptoed across the room to the door. *Please don't let anyone be waiting outside this time.* The last thing she needed was another confrontation. Eunice appeared to be open to working with her, but she wasn't sure she could trust her. And making the wrong decision could get her a bullet to the back of the head.

She hadn't been able to get a signal from her tent when she'd tried to call Ezekiel. When she'd wondered about it to Eunice, the other girl had told her it was because Reece used some sort of booster, but she didn't know a thing about it. The girl seemed to know what she was talking about though because when she got closer to the camper to make the call, it'd gone through without any problem.

She eased the door shut behind her as a Kid Rock song blasted from the phone she'd just returned. If she'd been a second later, she would've been standing there with it in her hand. Easing her way around the camper, she lingered near the window and listened as he answered the call, his voice groggy from sleep. He must've hit the button for speaker phone as someone else's voice rang through loud and clear.

"There's a couple of people down here asking about you. The man's mannerisms suggest he might be a cop, so I assume the girl with him is his partner. They didn't come right out and say they knew who you were, but I ferreted it out of them. They know your name and suspect your whereabouts."

"Did you get a name?"

"Malachi James."

An aggravated groan reached Becky, and she cringed inwardly. This was it. He'd kill her.

"I may know who that is. He's a park ranger near here. A little out of his jurisdiction down in West Virginia, isn't he?"

"Park ranger? Why would he care about you?"

Reece made a humming sound. "I may have a clue to that. It didn't occur to me when I met him. James is such a common name and Rebecca went back to her maiden name after Ezekiel's arrest, but she recommended we come to Worlds End to scout out properties nearby. Something tells me Becky Groves can tell me everything I need to know."

"You think?"

"The guy who went to prison, Ezekiel James. I'm betting this Malachi James is his son. And if so, I'd stake money on Rebecca being his mother. I'm not one-hundred percent positive, but I'll find out. Tonight. I have ways of making people talk. She'll find I'm quite persuasive."

Becky shut her eyes and sucked in a sharp breath. She'd seen Reece at his worst and didn't plan to hang around to endure an interrogation. It was time to make herself scarce. She needed to get out of Loyalsock State Forest. Taking the time to grab her things could be the difference between life and death. If she could get back to Worlds End, Malachi could still do something about Reece. He could take over. All it would take was a nudge in the right direction. Now. With no vehicle, no driver's license, and no sense of direction, escaping would be a challenge, but it was better than the alternative. Slipping away silently, she avoided her tent and found shelter in the woods. It wouldn't be long before the sun went down and the temperatures dropped. Darkness came early when you were deep in the woods.

WISPS OF SMOKE FROM the firepit burned Reece's eyes. He waved away the smoke and grabbed a fistful of Clarence's shirt. "Find Becky! She trusts you. Make her believe she's safe with you and get her back here." The expression on Clarence's face remained placid. The older man was unrattled by Reece's tirade. A trait that both impressed and annoyed him in equal parts.

"What if she won't come with me?"

"Bring her by force."

"And if I can't?"

"Dispose of the problem. One way or another, Rebecca Groves will cease to be an issue for me. Take care of her, or I'll take care of you. Got it?"

"Sure, boss. I'll handle Becky."

Reece plopped down on a log and stared at the glowing embers. They would fade in time. So would the community's memories of him. It was time to move on. They'd welcomed him, and he'd easily blended in with them, leaving the past behind, but the outside world threatened to infringe on the life he'd found.

A new identity in a faraway place was his best bet. Somewhere brimming with people where a man with a storied past could fade into the shadows of the skyscrapers. First, he needed a new identification. Papers proving he was someone he wasn't. Once he had those in hand, he'd disappear. He closed his eyes against thoughts of Dorcas and the twins. They couldn't join him where he was going. It was hard enough to disappear as a single man. Dragging along a family would prove tedious in the extreme. Besides, if he forced her to leave her community, she'd want answers, and he refused to answer to anyone but himself. Answering to his father was what got him into the mess he was in to begin with.

Chapter Twenty-One

Aggressive barking greeted Malachi and Cate when they arrived at Hector's place. He answered the door with a scowl. "Whatcha want?" A do-rag covered greasy dark hair that curled over his collar. The man kept his hold on the collars of two fierce dogs Malachi assumed were Dobermans.

"Was hoping to ask you a few questions about a community that used to be here."

"What for?"

"I lived there as a child."

"Give me a sec."

Hector came back several minutes later without the dogs, but they didn't quiet down. And he didn't invite them in. "What do you want to know?"

"I was taken from the community when the FBI raided it when I was a child, but from what I understand they reestablished themselves."

"That's true."

The dogs finally quieted down, and Malachi could once again hear himself think. "I believe my biological mother remains with them, so anything you can tell me would be a tremendous help."

"Oh. Sure. I get it now. You're looking for your mama." He pulled a pack of smokes from his shirt pocket, shook one loose, and lit it. "About a month ago, they up and left. Don't know where they went, but they're gone now."

"No idea where they might've gone?"

"Nah."

"Ever hear of a guy named Reece? I heard he's running things now." Malachi glanced around him. Something didn't sit right. Too quiet. Too still.

Hector took a drag of his cigarette and stared out at the mountain range in the distance. "Yeah. He was running things. Didn't much like people asking questions though."

"Any clue where he came from?"

"None. Look, I've got work to do."

"Sure. We'll get out of your way. Thanks for talking with us. If you think of anything more, give me a call." He turned to Cate. "Do you have a pen and paper?" She gave him a pen and a receipt. Malachi wrote his number on the back and handed it to him. "Thanks for your time."

Malachi opened the passenger door for Cate and a loud crack split the area. The bullet whizzed over them, missing his head by centimeters. He pushed Cate into the car. "Stay down."

"Is that gunfire?"

"Yeah."

"A hunter with bad aim?"

Another shot hit the rear windshield. Not hunters. Someone wanted to kill him or possibly just scare him. This was what happened when you asked too many questions in a quiet West Virginia mountain town. People didn't like questions, and they didn't like strangers. They'd protect their own even if their own didn't deserve their protection. "Get on the floor and stay there."

He looked toward the front door of the ranch house as he slammed the car into gear then sped down the gravel road and prayed God would protect Hector and his dogs. This wasn't his only experience with gunfire, but it was the first time the shooters had been aiming at him. A scene flashed before him of long guns aimed at the FBI who were there to take his father down. The community had lost a few of its own that long ago night, but they'd taken a few lawmen out in the melee. His father hadn't been convicted of their deaths. They'd tried him for them, but the charges hadn't stuck. The men who'd taken the shots had claimed he had no foreknowledge of their intentions. In other words, they lied.

Shaking off the memories, he turned to Cate. "You okay down there?"

"Someone is shooting at us!" Cate struggled to draw in a breath as she huddled on the floor of the passenger seat. "Why?"

"Don't know." He raced down streets dotted with potholes and ruts. A hairpin turn. A curve in the road. She might throw up if they didn't slow down soon. A left turn. "We're merging onto the highway. You can get back in your seat."

"Any clue who was shooting at us?" She clicked her seatbelt into place. Her mind spun. Certainly not a normal day at the office or out scouting den sites. If this was what life with Malachi was going to be like, she'd better get some practice shooting her handgun. It wasn't something she enjoyed, but her father and brothers had insisted she learn how to defend herself. They weren't wrong, but that powerful feeling of holding her Sig Sauer knowing she had the potential of taking a life wasn't something she relished. It made her a touch queasy every time she held it.

"I don't. All I do know is it couldn't have been Hector. He was standing in his doorway without a gun in his hand."

"You're not thinking it was Charlie, are you?"

"Could've been. Or he could've told someone we were looking. My father is another possibility."

"You think your own blood would try to kill you?"

"Might've wanted to scare me off. Or might've mentioned our being here to the wrong person. But don't be fooled. People can look you in the eye and say the nicest things all while planning your demise."

"What a lovely thought."

He shrugged.

Cate was grateful her outlook on life wasn't quite as grim as his. She'd been through her share of storms, but somehow she still believed in giving people the benefit of the doubt. Trusting until she'd been given a reason not to. Malachi's biological father's behavior in the past certainly justified his feelings for him now, but it was sad to see a family so broken. "I'm sorry that you can't trust your dad."

Malachi squeezed her hand. "Don't worry about it. He's not my dad, anyway. My foster dad is more of a father to me than Ezekiel James has ever been or ever will be. I'm here to prevent something awful from happening to my biological mother. I don't want her in my life, but I don't want her harmed, either. I told you about Maurice Moretti this morning. He could pose a threat to Becky and the rest of the community. I plan to keep him from harming them."

She nodded. "Hope we can stop him."

"We?"

"You didn't think I'd let you do this alone now that I know what you're dealing with, did you?"

"I think it's time for me to remove you from the equation. If I'd known it would be this dangerous to come here, I wouldn't have brought you with me. It's probably best if you avoid any further involvement in this whole mess."

She ignored the dismissal. He needed her help, and she wasn't about to back down from the threat. "And now you think he's in Pennsylvania?"

"I know he was. Whether he still is or not is the part I'm unsure of. He's definitely our poacher. I checked him into the cabin myself."

"Ugh."

"Got an email from Kevin this morning about a man's body being found in a lake near Dushore. They traced the guy to the wildlife trafficking. He was our buyer."

"And Reece was the seller?"

"Yep."

"I wish we would've caught them that night. We might've saved that man's life."

"Me too." He raked a hand through his hair while keeping his other hand on the wheel.

"And you think he's with your biological mother?"

"I do."

"This is beginning to make sense. Not in a good way." She tapped her fingers against the console. Inviting herself on this trip had been a spur of the moment crazy thing to do, but she was here now, and there was no way she'd leave Malachi to confront a cult led by a killer.

He blew out a breath. "I'll take you home if you don't want any part of my mess."

"I'm not going anywhere. I'm in this with you."

As SHE'D KNOWN IT would, the temperature dropped as night fell, and her teeth chattered to prove it. The outline of a structure in the distance looked promising. Possibly an old shack. Becky hugged her arms across her body and wished she'd worn warmer clothing that afternoon. But the warmth of the mid-March sunshine had tricked her into believing a light jacket would be enough. A shiver crawled up her spine as much from the night sounds as from the cold. Coyotes called. An owl hooted. An animal made a screeching sound similar to a woman's scream. None of it was comforting.

Her mind traveled back to the night she'd left home. Kicked out at twelve years old. She closed her eyes against the emotions the memories brought up. That first night had been spent on a park bench. It was three days later when a woman found her and brought her to Ezekiel. And from that time forward, she'd had a place she belonged. Until his arrest.

Reaching the wooden building, she shook her head. An old outhouse. Not the best shelter, but it would have to do. She had no other options. Inside, she found a half-rotten piece of plywood that formed the bench. Thankfully, it had gone unused long enough that there was no foul odor, only a deep earthy scent along with a bit of mustiness. There was enough room on the old plywood for her to curl up in the fetal position. She'd have to lay down her thin jacket, which would leave her without a covering, but it wasn't like there were any other options. It was the safest place she could find to spend the night.

She went outside and searched for something she could use to make the night more bearable. A hemlock stood nearby. She didn't have a knife to cut the branches, but with enough twisting back and forth, one finally came free. Two or three more and she'd have a way to make her temporary bed a touch softer. It was the best she could do under the circumstances.

Chapter Twenty-Two

Cate swiped the corner of her mouth with a paper napkin. "That pizza was delicious."

"It was cheap frozen pizza. Not exactly gourmet."

"It was supreme. Didn't you enjoy those tiny bits of bell pepper?"

"You don't know how to cook, do you?"

She laughed. "Would it be a deal breaker if I told you I eat Campbell's soup for dinner most nights?"

He tugged her hand, and she gave in and moved closer to him on the couch. "I can cook, so I'm not looking for a woman with gourmet cooking skills."

"No? Then what are you looking for in a woman?" A dangerous question to ask, but the words spilled out before she could stop them.

He tugged on one of her braids. “I find myself drawn to a woman with incredible intelligence, compassion, and a fondness for her family that she tries to hide behind annoyance.”

Scrunching up her nose, she pulled away slightly. “The annoyance is real. Honest to goodness, those brothers of mine are aggravating.”

He raised a brow. “Who said it was you that I was drawn to?” He winked, and heat flooded her face. She’d give anything to have the ability to turn off her blushes. “The woman I have in my sights has the cutest sprinkling of freckles across the bridge of her nose. Her eyes are a rich green color I don’t believe I’ve ever seen before. I could get lost in those eyes. Your turn. What are you looking for in a man?”

Turnabout was fair play, but she didn’t want to answer his question. Honesty would make her vulnerable. Even more so than she already was, but she wouldn’t leave him hanging. She gripped his hands a little tighter. “I’m looking for a guy who will cook for me, even if it’s frozen pizza.”

He rewarded her with a chuckle.

“It’d be great if he didn’t mind that my career path might take me away from home some nights.”

His eyes searched hers. She wished she knew what he was hoping to find, so she could be sure to convey it. “What else?”

“I’d love it if he liked me for me instead of for my family’s money.”

“And?”

“If I’m being honest, I think I’m falling for a man who fits all my requirements in addition to being handsome and making my heart race.”

He released her hands and cupped her face with his right

hand, rubbing his thumb along her jaw line. Then he traced her lips with his index finger. His head lowered to hers, and he kissed her, but the feather-light touch wasn't enough. She wanted more. "Falling for me, are you?"

"Don't get a big head. I could've been describing anyone."

"I don't think so. You're here with me. That's telling, Cate."

"Shut up and kiss me."

He obliged, and she lost herself in the sensations swirling through her body. Every part of her wanted to be closer to him, but before she could form a coherent thought, he pulled back and rested his forehead against hers. "You don't know what you do to me, woman."

Her lips curved upward. "I might have an idea."

"Keep those ideas to yourself. We need to cool things off before we get carried away. I'm going to go take a cold shower."

She didn't see the harm in a few kisses, but taking things slow was the wiser course.

He dropped a kiss on her nose. "We can watch a movie after. If you'd like."

Yes. She'd like to spend as much time with him as possible. Before long they'd be back in Pennsylvania in their separate towns and they'd go weeks without seeing each other again. She closed her eyes against the sudden burning behind them. Crying wouldn't solve anything. If they were going to be a couple, they'd have to find a way to see each other. And, as Jenna reminded her, Cate was the one with the financial means to make that happen. Should they want to get serious, she'd have to consider a move.

MALACHI REVELED IN THE feel of his arm around Cate's body. If they hadn't gotten away from Hector's place in time, Cate would've become collateral damage from his asking too many questions. A call to Hector confirmed he and his dogs were safe, but an uneasiness squeezed his chest tight. Someone wanted them to stop digging into Jade. Who? If the group remained in Pennsylvania, who was left to harass them? Or had they returned to West Virginia? It was more likely than not, but Reece wouldn't be wise to return with the FBI on his trail. Could his father be behind the shooting? He rubbed his forehead and tried to concentrate on the chick flick Cate found for them to watch.

He didn't know what the movie was called and hadn't caught much of the story. The delicious mix of apples and pears emanating from the gorgeous creature beside him brought a smile to his lips despite his frustration with earlier events. And that wasn't the only thing keeping him from concentrating on the film.

She reached for the remote and paused the movie. "What's on your mind? You seem distracted."

"Sharing what I'm thinking about will not help either of us right now."

"Do you regret me coming with you?"

"Not at all." Well, maybe a little. But no reason to speak it aloud. His discomfort with her being there had nothing to do with wanting her there. Getting shot at earlier reminded him that this investigation wasn't safe for either of them, and he didn't want to put her in harm's way again.

"Are you sure?"

"I promise."

She kissed him, and he let the need to be close to her overtake him for a moment. But after a few passionate kisses he pulled back and caught his breath, lifting a prayer for the Lord to help him overcome temptation. She unpaused the movie and rested her head on his shoulder.

Cate returned her attention to the television screen and absently ran her fingers up and down his arm. He forced himself to remain a gentleman and kept his hands to himself.

When the final credits rolled, he was both relieved and disappointed. The last thing he wanted to do was head to their separate bedrooms, but putting distance between them was necessary for his sanity. They should've rented a hotel with their own rooms preferably on different floors. That would've been smarter. Here they were sharing a house. Even if they weren't sharing a bedroom, it would be far too easy to give in to their mutual desire. From here on out, he'd keep a respectable distance. And heaven help him if that wasn't what she had in mind, too.

If she was wearing his ring, he wouldn't have to fight his physical reactions to her. He forced his mind back to the present and away from thoughts of making her his wife. She'd likely panic and think he was moving far too fast if she knew where his thoughts were going. Normal people didn't give their hearts away that fast.

She'd admitted to having feelings for him in a roundabout way, and she was demonstrating a definite attraction. Heaven knew he was falling for her. Her brother Grayson might be intimidating, but Malachi had no intention of letting him get in the way of what was developing between them.

Cate was incredible. Malachi never expected to find a woman he connected with the way he did with her. Everything about her appealed to him: from her being an animal lover who loved spending time outdoors, to her easy conversational style. Talking with her was comfortable. He felt compelled to share things with her nobody knew outside of his foster family. Although he had originally intended to go on this trip solo, it seemed fitting to have her accompanying him.

It might be too soon to speak aloud about a future together, but if he could convince her to take a chance on him, he hoped to spend the rest of his life attempting to make her happy, God willing. Closing his eyes, he lifted up a prayer asking the Lord for direction and the patience to wait on His timing.

Chapter Twenty-Three

Becky walked along the road until she heard a truck coming. It was risky to wave him down. What if it was one of Reece's men? She had to take the chance. She was too far from civilization to walk anywhere. Making it to Worlds End seemed plausible when she'd left the campsite, but she had no sense of direction and couldn't get herself there without assistance. When the vehicle drew closer she waved frantically, hoping the driver would slow. But he kept going, ignoring her obvious distress.

It was a good thirty minutes later before she heard another car. This time the driver stopped. "You need help?" The woman appeared to be in her fifties with long silvery hair and a warm smile.

"Yes, please. I was separated from my group. Is there any way you can get me to the park office at Worlds End?"

"Wow. You did more than get separated. You're nearly fifteen miles from where you need to be. Hop on in. It's in the opposite direction from where I'm going, but I'll take you there."

If the woman was willing to go out of her way, then she wasn't going to argue. She couldn't turn to Ezekiel. He'd been clear when they'd spoken on the telephone that he had no desire to rekindle their relationship. Nor did he wish to return to Jade. He went so far as to call it a cult. If it was, he'd been the founder, so she wasn't sure what that said about him.

Malachi would step up and protect her. Even without knowing her identity, she had sensed his desire to help. Once he understood who he was and where he belonged, he'd embrace her world, and he'd eliminate Reece.

Cate leaned back in her desk chair and stared out her office window. Something changed while they'd been in West Virginia. She tapped her pen on the arm of her chair. No. It wasn't her imagination. Something was different. There was an immediate connection when they'd met, but the past few days had solidified it. Now they had to figure out what to do about it. A budding relationship was one thing, but long-distance was another.

It felt so good watching a movie with him beside her, but they wouldn't have opportunities like that often. When he came to see her, he'd have a long ride home. Even if they met in the middle, they'd both have a distance to drive to get back home.

And at dusk they'd be worried about deer.

She sucked in a breath of stale air. Thinking about all the things that could go wrong was borrowing trouble. Her mother would've told her to pray about it and turn her fears over to God. That was something she hadn't done in a long time. It wasn't as if she didn't pray, but those quick pleas were sent up spur of the moment when she had an urgent desire to ask for His help. Getting down on her knees and pouring her heart out was a thing of the past. When she'd been locked in that hidden room inside of the Ricketts Estate, it was the first time in her life she'd felt as if God had abandoned her.

When her mother died, she'd accepted the loss knowing her mother was safe in the arms of the Lord who loved her, but why had He allowed her friends to go through what they had? And if her brothers and Samantha hadn't rescued her, would she feel like part of her soul had been stripped away? That's how Brittany described it. Emmaline seemed to take everything in stride and moved on with her life, but Brittany had been taken as the wife of a cold-blooded psychopath. Cate couldn't understand why God had allowed it. Why hadn't He helped Cate save her closest friends from that monster? Tears slipped past her lashes and she swiveled her chair around, dropped her pen on her desk, and grabbed a tissue to dab at her eyes.

But Cate had been rescued. Samantha had shown up in the nick of time. Was that answered prayer? Was she blaming God for the actions of evil men? Why was it so hard to get back to fellowshipping with the Lord the way she had before her time at the Ricketts Estate?

Dwelling on the past wasn't helping. There was work to be done. Virginia expected a telephone call this morning, and that meant finding the strength to dial the number. A task that sounded so simple in theory, but it wasn't easy for her. She rested her head on the desk and sobbed. Normal people didn't panic over making a telephone call. It was times like these when she missed her mother the most. And her relationship with her Savior.

A text came through, and she smiled at the Yoda meme Samantha sent. She made a fabulous big sister. Maybe God did care about her. Somehow, Sam was always there when she was needed. That couldn't be a coincidence.

She sucked in a sharp breath and gathered her strength, then dialed the number. Her boss answered on the third ring just as she was about to hang up. "Hello?"

"Hi, Virginia. It's Cate."

"Oh! I'm glad you called. We got a tip from a civilian that there is a bear denned up in Loyalsock State Forest. I need you and your team to check it out to see if it's a sow and whether or not she has cubs. If she does, it's perfect for placing the final cub from Worlds End."

"That's great news." A smiled tugged the corners of her mouth. Even her phone phobia couldn't ruin this for her. Placing Bruce so close to where he'd been taken would be perfect. Her team was finishing up a project they started while she was away, but she could check it out on her own and then bring them in once she knew what they were dealing with.

"As long as your team can get there this week, it should be a go. If not, we'll have a conservation officer tag the bear denned there."

"We'll prioritize that site since it's ideal for the cub."

"Good to hear. Let me know what you find when you scout the location."

MALACHI SLOGGED THROUGH THE rain and mud looking for the missing fisherman. Probably took shelter, but his wife called claiming he should've been home hours earlier. For all he knew the man had decided to stop somewhere on his way home and was chatting with a buddy, but he'd seen enough instances of people being swept away in the fast-moving creek waters to take the lady's concerns seriously.

A flash of orange in the distance caught his eye, and he trudged toward the bright spot. When he neared it, he recognized it as a ball cap. It rested on a log. Not their missing man. Something reflective snagged his attention. A fishing pole with a flashy lure tied on it leaned against a tree, but still no sign of the man to whom they belonged. Shaking his head, he surveyed the area. Nothing to indicate where he'd gone.

Malachi had never been one for fishing this time of year. He preferred to wait until trout season opened. Not only was it better fishing, it was safer with more people around.

The wind carried a faint sound. He strained to identify its source. His feet moved downstream as he recognized the shout for help. Thirty feet farther, he found the source of the noise—an elderly man clinging to a tree branch as water rushed around him. He called it in and moved closer. "I'm going to get you out there, Mr. Gray."

The man didn't respond. Probably had a sore throat from screaming for help. And too worn out to do anything more than cling to his lifeline.

Malachi pulled a rope from his backpack and tied himself to

a tree. He ventured into the creek, fighting against the strength of the rushing water with each step. After hooking himself to the other man, he helped him to the shore. "The EMTs should be here shortly. You okay to walk?"

The man struggled for breath, but he nodded. "Thank you. How did you know where to find me?"

"Mr. Gray, if you hadn't told your wife when to expect you home, we wouldn't have found you in time. She called in a panic, and gave us an idea of where you planned to fish."

"Celia. A good wife is a blessing from the Lord."

In that moment, Malachi didn't doubt the truth of the man's words. Without someone waiting at home, Melvin Gray likely would've been carried to his death once he grew too weak to keep hanging on.

Malachi slapped the back of the ambulance when the doors closed. When it pulled away with Mr. Gray inside, he drove back to the office. A good wife. Yes. That was what Mr. Gray had, and maybe, just maybe it was what God had in store for him, too.

Quitting time couldn't come soon enough. He changed into dry clothes and poured himself some coffee, but what he wanted more than anything in that moment was a long hot shower. Kevin sauntered into the back office, frowning. "That lady who made the report about the bear cubs a couple of weeks back is at the front desk demanding to see you."

Chapter Twenty-Four

Cate parked her truck and glanced at her cell. She should've texted before leaving the house. No service. Maybe the message would send if she hiked through a spot with service. Otherwise, she could show up at the office and hope Malachi was working. They hadn't spoken since arriving back in Pennsylvania two days ago. On her end, she hadn't wanted to appear desperate by texting right away, but she wasn't sure what his excuse was. Maybe he was busy. He had mentioned a spring training game he was looking forward to watching. Restoring her communion with the Lord required trust on her part. Trust that His timing was perfect, and He knew what she needed better than she did.

Cate: I'm nearby. Loyalsock State Forest.

Want to meet for dinner?

As expected, her screen kept blinking the 'sending...' message, so she stuffed her phone into her coat pocket and grabbed her backpack. She probably should've let someone know where she was headed and when to expect her back, but she'd scouted sites alone plenty of times in the past. And this one was a priority. It would take time to assemble her team. Time she didn't have.

A quick trek in and out of the woods, and she'd be on her way to the park office at Worlds End to see if Malachi was available for a meal. Her stomach growled at the thought. All she'd had for breakfast was a protein bar and a thermos of coffee.

-five minutes later, when she arrived at the spot indid by the coordinates given to them by the hikers, she squatted before what appeared to be a discarded truck cap. How it could've found its way so deep into the woods, she couldn't begin to guess, but it'd been there for ages. Debris covered it to the point where it looked like it belonged. Part of the natural landscape. A sow snoozed in the makeshift den beneath it with a single cub. It would be the perfect place to bring the final cub. The mama bear would easily accept Bruce as her own when she awakened in a few short weeks. If they managed to get him there in time. But Cate didn't expect that to be a problem.

After taking a few photographs, she checked her phone. Still no service. She stuffed it into her pocket and picked her way over the rough terrain until she was back on the trail. She'd hiked for about ten minutes when she tripped over a rock. She leaned against a tree to steady herself. Smoke rose in the distance. Forest fire or camper? March wasn't popular for camping, but maybe a hiker lit a fire to make lunch. She veered off the trail, climbed atop a large rock and pulled out her binoculars. Tents and a couple of campers scattered along the edges of what appeared to be an old logging road. A fire blazed in the center of camp. As far as she could tell from the forest map, this wasn't anywhere near any authorized camping areas.

It wasn't a forest fire. That was a blessing. The bears and other woodland creatures should be safe enough.

She marked the waypoint on her phone, intent on reporting the visitors. Then hopped down off the rock and swiped her hands across her jeans. A metallic click behind her made her blood run cold. She'd know that sound anywhere.

Lifting up a prayer for protection, she forced her breath to steady.

"Move. Nice and slow." The voice was male. Appalachian accent, but heavier than what one usually heard in these parts. If she had to guess, she'd say West Virginia. She closed her eyes as the obvious explanation hit her. This was the cult Malachi was trying to find. They hadn't gone far from Worlds End at all. Just down the street while they'd been searching in West Virginia.

If they were the same people who'd shot at them, she couldn't go with them or she might not make it out of these woods alive.

"I said move." He pressed the barrel against the base of her skull and she complied, taking a step forward. Going against the man now might cost her life, but if she did as he asked, God might provide a means of escape. If not, she knew the verse. Absent from the body. Present with the Lord. One way or another, she'd be all right.

MALACHI CAME THROUGH THE doors, looking a little scruffier

than the last time she saw him. But after spending the night in an outhouse, she didn't look her best either. She chewed on her bottom lip and rubbed her hands along her skirt. "I didn't know where else to go."

"What happened?"

"I overheard a phone call. I'm pretty sure Reece means to kill me." She picked at a loose thread on her coat.

He raised an eyebrow. "Kill you? Why would your boyfriend kill you?"

"I'm not in a relationship with him. He's the head of our community now, but he shouldn't be. It's not his place."

"Let's go into the back and talk." He held the door for her and she preceded him to his desk and sank into a chair. The same one she'd occupied on her last visit.

"I need to go to West Virginia. I can't stay here."

"Whoa there. Let's take this one step at a time, okay?" He sighed. "Where did you go when you left the cabin here?"

"The state forest."

"Which one?"

"Loyalsock."

"Would you be able to show us where you were, exactly?"

Becky shook her head. "I don't think so, no." She could find her way back there, but she wasn't going back. West Virginia was where she belonged. Ezekiel was there. He'd make everything all right. His words replayed in her mind. 'I'm not the man I once was, Rebecca. Don't come.' Maybe his phones were being tapped. The FBI was crafty. And he would've learned from his mistakes. Now that he was out, he'd want to lead again. With her beside him. If not, what was the point in any of it? Her life was worthless without him.

Unless, she could convince Malachi. That idea no longer

seemed to fit. Her son didn't belong in the community. He may have been born there, but he didn't fit the mold. And Zeke called it a cult. Were they a cult? They didn't follow a man; they followed the gods. But the gods communicated through the jade to a man. Could it all be one big hoax? No. Not a chance. This had been her life since she was twelve years old and nobody was going to take it from her. She wouldn't accept that her entire life had been based on a lie.

"You can stay at my place tonight. I have a spare room."

The other park ranger moved into her field of vision. "You can't do that, Malachi. It goes against regulations. We need to find a shelter somewhere who can take her."

Malachi locked eyes with the other man. "I'm not placing my mother in a shelter."

The man took two steps back. "I knew there was something you weren't telling me that day we checked out the cabin. Your mother, huh?" He shoved his hands in his pockets. "In that case, you should offer her a room." He sighed. "When you decide to trust me with the whole story, call me. I'm clocking out."

A look of anguish flickered across Malachi's features, and Becky's chest tightened painfully. He'd known who she was but chose not to acknowledge their relationship until now. Why? Maybe he thought she wouldn't want him to know who she was.

"I'm getting off my shift, too. Why don't you wait outside for me?" He frowned.

CHAPTER TWENTY-FIVE

MALACHI UNLOCKED THE FRONT door. "Wait here a minute. I need to put Titan in his crate so he doesn't jump on you."

"Titan?"

"He's a Bernese Mountain dog."

At her confused look, he clarified. "He's a large dog. He's trained, but I don't want to take any chances. If he were to jump on you, he'd knock you off your feet." Once he'd taken a minute to greet his furry friend, he grabbed a cookie knowing it would encourage him to willingly get in his crate. "Good boy."

He returned to the front door and held the door for Becky to enter. "We can talk after we've both gotten cleaned up." He showed her to the guest room. "I don't have any women's clothing, but I might be able to scrounge up a pair of sweatpants and a sweatshirt you can wear until you have a chance to wash your clothes. There's a bathroom down the hall. Take your time. I'll cook up some dinner. Once you're settled, we can let Titan out, so you can get to know each other."

Once he was inside his own bedroom, he shut the door and leaned his head against it. He glanced at his bed longingly before moving into the adjoining bathroom. A shower was a must before he could relax. When he set his phone on the counter, he noticed a text from Cate asking him about getting together for dinner. It must've come through when he was changing clothes at the office.

Malachi: Sorry I missed your message. If you're still in town, maybe you could come by the house for dinner. There are some new developments I'd like to share.

He waited several minutes, but when no response came, he set down his cell. Five minutes later, he finished toweling off and threw on a pair of jeans and a long-sleeved t-shirt then grabbed his cell, flopped down on his bed, and stared at the ceiling. A quick glance at his phone showed there was still no response from Cate.

Malachi: You there, Cate?

He stared at his phone for a good two minutes. No answer. After checking his email, he looked to see if she'd responded. Nothing.

Malachi: If you can answer me, please do. I'm worried.

A bark reminded him he'd left Titan in his crate, so he headed to the family room to let him out. Becky sat on the sofa. Oddly enough, Pixie was curled up in her lap purring. His cat didn't take to many people, so he wasn't sure what to make of that.

"I'm going to need to let Titan out. Are you afraid of dogs?"

Her eyes widened, but she didn't voice any fears. He spoke calmly to the dog and opened his crate. Titan sat in front of Becky, clearly expecting the same reception he'd received from Cate, but that wasn't going to happen. Becky tentatively held her hand out for him to sniff, but then quickly jerked it back and once again buried her fingers in the cat's fur. Satisfied that the introduction had gone as well as could be expected, he headed into the kitchen with Titan at his heels.

Maybe cooking dinner would prove to be the distraction he needed. The search for ingredients to put together a decent meal was rewarded with chicken and vegetables. Twenty minutes later, the smell of honey-garlic chicken stir fry sizzling on the burner brought Becky into the kitchen.

"Something smells good."

He set out plates for three, in case Cate showed up, then scooped some rice onto two of the plates and topped it with the stir fry. "Dinner's ready."

"Who is the other plate for?" Becky asked.

"My girlfriend."

"That redhead girl I saw in the park office a couple of weeks ago?"

"That's her. Yes."

"She's pretty. Does she live here with you?"

He clenched his jaw tight. Cate was none of her business, but saying so would be rude. "Yep, she is pretty. She has her own place in State College, but she's working near here today." After silently asking God to help him be the man he'd created him to be, he said Grace. Becky's demeanor made it clear she was uncomfortable with prayer, but they were in his house. And in his house, God reigned supreme.

They ate the remainder of the meal in silence. When he finished eating, he glanced at his phone again. Still no response. Her phone may have died.

He could check with her brothers. Heaven knew those two kept close tabs on her. He didn't want to appear overbearing and overprotective when he knew she had enough of that in her life. But, on the other hand, if she was in some kind of trouble, he wanted to help. However, if she was held up at work and he made a huge big deal of it, she wouldn't take his overreaction well.

If he was smart, he'd focus on what he was going to do about Becky instead of worrying so much about Cate. But his internal alarms were shouting a warning. Something was wrong, and he couldn't ignore it.

THE STRANGER HAD EYES like ice. Cold and distant. She assumed he was Reece Mclean aka Maurice Moretti. He used two lengths of rope to bind her ankles and wrists then stuffed her into a tent. "Scream, and I'll shoot you."

The fact that he didn't gag her told her nobody who would care would hear her screams even if he hadn't threatened her into silence. None of her self-defense courses or shooting range time prepared her for someone sneaking up behind her and pointing a gun at her skull. When she'd been held captive the last time, she hadn't been able to save herself, but a voice inside told her that if she wanted to survive this, she'd need to find a way to do just that.

Once Reece was gone, she sat up and scooted around. She could move, albeit not easily.

Positioning herself so she could see through the crack in the tent door, she watched the people milling about. Very few people spoke, and she assumed those brave enough to talk were the ones in charge. They looked like they were preparing for war. Men loaded guns into a camper. Women carried boxes to a truck. She couldn't tell what the boxes contained, but she highly doubted it was used clothing destined for Goodwill.

If she managed to get herself out of the tent, someone would notice. And, she'd likely get herself shot. She'd been hoping to sneak away while they slept, but it looked like they were leaving in a hurry. The question was would they kill her first, take her with them, or leave her behind. None were great options, but she preferred the last. Unlikely they'd leave her. Her death wouldn't mean much to a man who killed people for a living. One of her classmates had done a presentation about the Moretti family a few years back. From what he'd said, the younger Moretti was trained by his father. Having had a supportive and loving family, she couldn't wrap her mind around the idea of a father who would teach his young son how to take the lives of other human beings for profit.

But her emotional response to his upbringing was a concern she needed to set aside. Now it was her life at stake, and she needed to find a way to survive.

The zipper moved, and she scooted herself as far away from the opening as possible.

A man's face appeared in the tent door. His sneer didn't offer any comfort. "Ready to go?" He grabbed her feet and yanked her free from the relative safety of the flimsy canvas. Her body bounced on the hard ground, and her skull made contact with a rock. She couldn't rub the sore spot, not with her hands bound. The man showed no sign of concern over his own brutality. "Reece said for me to take you to Clarence, but you are a pretty little thing. Maybe if I ask nice, he'll let me keep you alive."

"Micky!" Another man appeared beside him. "What are you doing?"

"Getting the ginger for you, Clarence."

"Reece said to bring the woman to me, not to drag her off like you're some kind of caveman." The man called Clarence squatted beside her and ran a knife along the ropes binding her ankles. "So you can walk." He smiled. "We're getting in that truck over there." He gestured toward a blue Dodge pickup that had seen better days. It showed more rust than paint on the back doors and she guessed it wasn't road legal. She could picture the bed detaching itself from the cab if it hit a large pothole.

"What's your name?"

She ignored the question, having no desire to participate in a back-and-forth with her captors. Little did they know this wasn't her first abduction, and she'd had plenty of time since then for thinking about all the things she would've done differently if given the chance. Looked like this was her opportunity to prove to herself that she wasn't weak and pathetic.

"Cat got yer tongue, sweetheart?" Clarence chuckled.

Chapter Twenty-Six

As he drove them down the old logging road, Clarence muttered under his breath, "You'll be out of here soon. No worries."

A strong odor of gasoline filled the cab. Could be a leak. She studied his profile. "Is Reece planning to kill me?"

"Absolutely."

"Then it seems worrying is my best course of action at this point."

"I'm not planning to let him kill you."

"And you expect me to believe that?"

"I need you to help me find Becky Groves."

"She's not here?"

"No. Ran off."

"And he wants her back." It wasn't a question. Maurice Moretti—if that was who this Reece Mclean really was—wouldn't want to leave loose ends. If Becky knew things he didn't want her sharing, she was certain he wouldn't hesitate to snuff out her life.

There was a firm set to his jaw, and he scratched at the stubble covering it. "He does, yes. But so do I. Rebecca belongs to me."

"If Becky hadn't run off, I'd be dead. She's the only reason your leader kept me alive."

"Ding. Ding. Ding. The girl wins a prize." He grinned. "You gonna help me find her or not?"

"Do you intend to harm her?" She didn't know where the woman might've gone, so she couldn't help him even if she wanted to, but her guess was they wanted her to lead them to Malachi in hopes he would lead them to his mother. Cate wouldn't allow herself to be used as a pawn in their deadly game. No. She wouldn't help them find Malachi's mother.

Her question went unanswered.

Clarence rapped his knuckles against the steering wheel. "We're going to start at the park office. Worlds End. They're not open, but we'll be there when they arrive in the morning. If your boyfriend wants you to live, he'll tell me where Rebecca has gone. And if he doesn't show up for work, you'll give me directions to his place."

"He won't go for it. I'm nobody to him."

"Don't downplay your worth, sweetheart. It might get you killed prematurely."

Cate directed her gaze to the heavens and lifted a prayer asking God to give her the strength to fight when the time came, so that she wouldn't make things worse for Malachi and Becky.

Malachi's thumb traced the old-fashioned compass keyring Cate left in his car. A gift from her grandpa she'd said. It had fallen off her coat zipper, and she'd stuffed it into the cup holder. He dialed Grayson's number. Another thing she'd left with him. Just in case. He hadn't expected to need it so soon. And he might be overreacting. If that were the case, there was no doubt he'd suffer Cate's wrath, but ignoring possible danger wasn't wise either.

"Garrison Security." A calm female voice answered.

"I was hoping to talk to Grayson Garrison." He paced his bedroom not wanting to alert Becky to the possible trouble just yet.

"I'm sorry, he had all his mobile calls forwarded to the office as he plans to be unreachable until next Monday."

"This is about his sister Cate. You must have some way to get him on the line."

"Let me take your number, and someone will return your call immediately."

His heart raced as he left his phone number. Dropping to the bed, he stared at the ceiling and lifted up a prayer, but before he could say amen, a call came in. "Hello."

"This is Gavin Garrison. You were trying to reach my brother about Cate."

"Yes. This is Malachi James. Cate and I have been seeing each other. I know it's only been a few hours, but something tells me that she's in trouble."

"Back up. You're not making any sense."

"Cate sent me a text this afternoon saying she was in the area. She planned to hike out to the location she'd been given of a bear den. Once she finished her work, she wanted to grab dinner with me before she returned to State College."

"By herself? She was hiking to a bear den alone?"

"That was my understanding. Besides the possible danger with wildlife encounters, there are a few places in Loyalsock with sheer cliff drop-offs. And the temperatures can drop significantly in the elevations this time of year."

"You didn't try to stop her?"

"I didn't know she was going until it was too late. Besides, would she have listened?"

"What time did you get the text?"

"That's the strange thing. It didn't come through until four in the afternoon. If I were to venture a guess, I'd say she mustn't have had service when she sent the text, but I can't say for sure. Maybe she started her hike that late."

"Doesn't sound like her."

"I didn't think so either."

"If Cate thought you didn't get her message, she might've headed home."

"I tried her cell and her landlady. It might be too soon to worry, but I'm afraid something may have happened."

"Do you have the coordinates for the bear den by any chance?"

"I don't, but I may be able to get them. Cate's supervisor is a woman named Virginia Vaughn. I'll give her a call. She'll probably have that information or be able to get it for us."

"Do that. What's your address?"

He rattled it off.

"I'll be at your house in about thirty minutes."

"Take your time. You wouldn't want to hit a deer."

Gavin made a non-committal sound and disconnected the call.

Malachi stared into the darkness outside his window and

wondered if he'd made the right decision calling in Cate's brothers. When Kevin had left the office, things between them weren't great, but Malachi knew he could count on his fellow ranger despite that. He sucked in a breath to steady himself and called Kevin's cell. The younger man answered with a "Yo." Malachi blinked away his annoyance at the kid's lack of telephone manners.

"Hey, Kev."

"What's up?"

"Do you think you can get me the phone number for Virginia Vaughn? She's with the Game Commission."

"Sure. Thought you were off work tonight?"

"I am. This is a personal matter."

"You want me to call you back with it or hold while I get it?"

"Will it be fast?"

"Should be."

"Then I'll hold. Thanks."

Less than a minute later he had the number and was dialing it. Within five he had the location, but he had to wait for Gavin. Night hiking to a bear den without backup would be beyond stupid, so he'd stay here and twiddle his thumbs.

It hadn't been ten minutes since he hung up with Gavin that his doorbell rang. Cate? He threw open the door hoping it was her. Grayson Garrison.

"My brother said Cate's missing."

"You got here quick."

"I was in the area."

Malachi handed the man his cell.

"You haven't heard anything since this last text?"

"Not a word. I've called, texted, checked with her landlady. Everything I could think to do."

"Did you get the location?"

"I did."

"Let's go. Gavin can meet us there."

Malachi slung his backpack on his shoulder and grabbed his coat. "One second." He returned to his bedroom and grabbed Cate's compass from where he'd left it and stuffed it into his pocket then sought out his house guest. "Becky, I'll be back at some point. In the meantime, just hang out here. I'm expecting Cate's other brother Gavin. Just give him the note I left on the table. He'll probably be here shortly. It's better if you stay in tonight, so make yourself comfortable." Not that she had anywhere else to go. It sounded like it was here or nowhere. There weren't any shelters in the area.

When he made his way outside, Grayson already had his Bronco running.

BECKY HAD HOPED TO spend time with her son. But he'd chosen to search for Cate instead of reuniting with her. She couldn't fault him. Not really. It'd been her who abandoned him first. Twenty-four years was a long time to go without seeing your mother. She should know. It had been more than thirty years since she'd seen her own parents. And she wouldn't be as nice to them as Malachi was being to her.

She took advantage of her son's unexpected absence. It was an opportunity to find out more about him. A little snooping was in order. His bathroom cabinets revealed the usual things. An old prescription bottle for an antibiotic, razors, soap. Nothing earth-shattering there. His nightstand produced some books, a pack of tissues, and a pistol. That could come in handy if she had to leave in a hurry. She slid out the magazine. Fully loaded. Plus one in the chamber. She stuffed the gun into her pocket. If he were here, he'd probably agree she should have it. After all, he knew she was in danger. Reece planned to kill her.

When she tripped over the length of the straight-leg sweatpants Malachi had given her, she murmured an expletive. They swam on her, but thankfully, there was a tie in the front which kept them in place.

Her search took her into the family room where she found a briefcase. Inside, she discovered a photograph of Reece. It wasn't a recent one. The name below it was unfamiliar, but she'd have known that face anywhere. Scanning the page, she caught a few words. FBI. Warrant. She wasn't the best at reading. Missing out on high school hadn't done her any favors when it came to that, but she knew all about the FBI. They were the ones who took Ezekiel away from her. As far as she was concerned, they were the enemy. But so was Reece. The question was which enemy was more of a threat at the moment. It seemed like the answer was Reece, but she wasn't certain about that. The FBI was evil. Horrid even. Why would a government agency break up her family? There was no good justification for what they'd done.

The doorbell put an end to her search. After stuffing the papers back where she'd found them, she answered the door to a handsome young man and a dark-haired woman. Resigned to playing hostess, she put on her usual plastic smile.

"Hi. I think I'm supposed to put the dog in his crate. Give me a sec." She opened the cage door, and the giant animal went inside without complaint. She'd expected him to give her a hard time. Back at the front door, she gestured for them to come inside. “Sorry about that.”

When Malachi had left her there, he’d told her to expect a man named Gavin, but hadn’t mentioned anything about the female.

“Is Malachi here?” Gavin asked.

“Grayson came, and they left to go check out a bear den. They said something about you meeting them there.”

“Do you know where they went?”

“He left a note for you on the table.”

Gavin looked at the woman. “You stay here with her. I’m sorry, what is your name again?”

“I’m Becky Groves. Malachi’s mother.” Probably not something Malachi wanted these strangers to know, but what did it matter. They’d find out eventually if she stuck around long.

“Sam, stay with Becky in case we need someone to go online or call in backup. Phones get wonky in the Pennsylvania Wilds.”

The woman laughed and rolled her eyes then turned to Becky. “I’m a park ranger. You’d think my hubby would realize I didn’t need a reminder about spotty cell service.” At least that explained what the woman was doing here. She was the missing girl’s sister-in-law.

Becky smiled, but sincerely wished that Samantha would tag along with her husband and leave her alone to continue her search. Now that she’d uncovered the photo of Reece, she wanted to find out why Malachi had it.

Chapter Twenty-Seven

There was no comfort for Malachi in the fact that Cate's brothers were as concerned about her disappearance as he was. He'd been hoping this was something she did, and that they'd tell him there was nothing to worry about. Of course, Cate had warned him they were beyond protective, so that might explain Grayson showing up in record time.

Leaving Becky alone in his house didn't sit right. But what choice did he have? Cate could be in danger. Everything was likely fine.

The air was cold and crisp and the overcast sky provided little light as they trudged through the forest using only their headlamps to illuminate the path before them.

They had hiked a mile or so through the pitch blackness

when Grayson stopped. “This is the spot.”

Malachi pulled out his night vision binoculars and used them to search the area. “Over there.” He squatted near the rectangular shape. It took a few seconds to register what he was looking at. “It’s a truck cap. The bear made her den beneath it. Put your hand here.” He gestured to the opening.

“Wow. You can feel her heat. That’s cool.”

“It is, isn’t it?”

“How did that decrepit piece of junk find its way here?”

“There are abandoned logging roads everywhere in these woods. Someone must’ve driven it back here at some point. Looks like it’s been here for years though.”

“I didn’t see any roads.”

“Most of them aren’t usable. There are trees growing through the middle of all of them, but a few can still be traversed if you’re determined enough. But I don’t see Cate anywhere. The good news is there are no signs of a struggle either.”

“Ah.” Gray looked around again. “You’re right.”

“It’s hard to tell in the dark. Maybe we can find some evidence she’s been here.” He shone his flashlight near the cap. “Footprints. Small enough to be female. Likely hers.”

“Do you think we can follow her trail?”

An owl made its presence known with a series of hoots. One of many creatures that hunted these woods at night. “I doubt it. It’s too dark. Maybe at first light.”

“Then I suppose we should get comfortable. You have a tent in that pack?”

“I do.”

“Knew you were a boy scout.”

He left that alone. He’d never been a boy scout, but a park ranger should never be in the wilderness without emergency supplies. Especially when they're expecting trouble. Once he had the tent assembled, he looked at himself and then over at Cate's brother. It was going to be a tight squeeze for two grown men, but they'd make it work.

CATE TRIED TO STRETCH her back. Her captor had reclined her seat for her, so she could get some rest, but sleep was evasive. Not unexpected considering her circumstances. Her wrists were rubbed raw from attempting to remove the ropes binding them, and every muscle in her body ached. The past twelve hours brought her back into a nightmare she'd rather not relive. Yet, here she was. Abducted again. It was almost unfathomable.

She closed her eyes and lifted a prayer. That's what Malachi would do. It's also what her landlady had encouraged. And right now, God was her only hope. If He didn't somehow make sure for her, she'd be in trouble. And so would Malachi. Who knew what their plans were for him when he arrived at work in the morning? They were parked in the lot outside of the park office, and the sun would rise shortly. Time wasn't on her side.

A loud snore came from the seat beside her, and she tried once more to find something in the vehicle to cut her ropes with before he awakened. He might speak kinder than the man who dragged her from the tent, but she didn't trust him. If he was on her side, she'd already be free.

Reece had planned to be gone before daybreak, but before he could go, he needed to take care of a few loose ends. He watched Dorcas sleep. Such a sweet girl. No guile. She truly believed that some useless piece of jade had mystical powers and could call out to the gods. It was ridiculous, but it did come in handy when he needed to control the mass of followers in the community. They'd believed he could communicate with the gods through a stone even though he didn't have the stupid gem in his possession. Truth was, the original stone they followed disappeared around the time Ezekiel James went to prison. His best guess was that the feds confiscated it as evidence of his crimes, but nobody seemed to know for sure. Probably nothing more than a cheap bit of chert. Certainly didn't hold the value these crazies believed it did.

If God was out there somewhere, He would put a stop to all the idol worship, wouldn't He? His grandmother had tried to teach him about a one true God, but his father would have none of it.

He'd taken him with him to work before he was old enough to ride a bicycle. By the time he started middle school, he was manning the sniper rifle.

Maybe his granny had been right, but it never made sense to him. Why would an all-powerful God allow His creation to fawn over false gods? Why not destroy them all? Start over again? He shook his head at the thought. The idea of a world created by an omnipotent being was a fairytale he'd never ascribed to, and today wouldn't be the day when that changed. Even if God was out there somewhere, He wouldn't want anything to do with Reece. No. He was beyond saving.

If he was heading for destruction, he'd take as many of these wackos with him as he could. Dorcas and the twins would live.

She would find a way to start over somewhere else once he was gone. He shook his head. Why was he kidding himself? If she found out what he'd been up to, she'd despise him. Maybe that was what she needed. Hate fueled action. If he forced her to watch him kill Becky and her useless son, then maybe she'd realize he was no good. That would force her to move on. Continue living once he was gone. He'd keep an eye on her from afar though. If another man touched her, that man would die.

Slipping from bed, he stepped outside. On the fourth ring, Clarence finally answered. "Where were you?"

"I'm at the park office waiting for Becky's kid to show up."

"Forget that. You're needed here. Bring the redhead back. We'll deal with Becky's kid later."

Chapter Twenty-Eight

At first light, Malachi sat up and tapped Gray on the shoulder. When Grayson immediately reached for his weapon, he raised his hands in the air. "It's just me."

"Sorry."

When they exited the tent, a man who looked like a younger version of Grayson sat leaning against a tree with his long legs stretched out before him. "I'm guessing you're Gavin."

"And you're Malachi?"

"In the flesh. When did you get here?"

"After you'd settled in for the night."

"Why didn't you wake us?" Gray asked.

"Didn't seem like there was room for three."

Malachi nodded. It was true, but they would've figured

something out rather than leave the man out in the elements all night. It had remained dry. A blessing. March weather was unpredictable giving them anything from sixty-degree sunshine to sleet and snow. Heavy rains were frequent occurrences. A downpour left two inches in its wake less than a week prior.

"My wife is at your house. Didn't think you'd mind if she hung out with your mom."

His mom. No, she was his biological mother, not his mom. No question about that, but it wasn't something he needed to get into with someone he barely knew. "Your wife is welcome at my house. It'll be good to have someone there keeping an eye on my mother."

Gavin laughed. He probably thought Malachi was joking.

They packed up the tent then Malachi threw protein bars to each of the Garrison men. "Eat. Then we'll see if we can track Cate."

"Boy scout." Gray unwrapped his and took a giant bite.

Malachi shook his head and rolled his eyes. The bland energy bar tasted like cardboard, but it would provide him with enough nutrition to keep him going. With the daylight on their side, they were easily able to identify Cate's tracks.

"Here." Gavin reached for a twig and used it to pick up a scrap of fabric. "This could be something."

Malachi studied the ground nearby. "This looks like it might be a women's boot print, but it's hard to say for sure."

"Wait. Look." Gray pointed to what looked like it could be a trail. "There are a few tracks leading away. Maybe she did leave the woods. In which case, where could she have gone?"

Malachi swallowed hard. The prospect of her tangling with a bear was terrifying, but the idea that something else kept her from calling didn't leave him feeling much better. He didn't believe she would've blown him off intentionally, which left something or someone preventing her from contacting him. He followed along behind the brothers as they traversed the trail.

"Wait." Malachi stopped. He wasn't sure what it was, but something didn't feel right. Then he smelled it. Smoke. "Someone has a campfire near here. We need to find it."

Gavin came to an abrupt stop. "You're right. It's faint, but I smell it."

"There is no authorized camping in this area, right?" Gray asked.

"I'm not certain, but I don't think so."

"Don't you work here?" Gavin asked.

Malachi shook his head. "This is Loyalsock State Forest. I work for Worlds End State Park. We all work for DCNR, but we're separate entities."

"Let's figure out where it's coming from." Gray wet a finger and held it up to figure out wind direction.

Malachi narrowed his eyes. "I'm not sure that'll help."

"Worth a shot." Gavin shrugged.

Becky chewed on her ragged fingernails as she stood over the sleeping woman. During her snooping last night, she'd found the map she'd left for Malachi packed away in his papers. She doubted Malachi's girlfriend had somehow stumbled on the community, but when Samantha called her father-in-law before she turned in for the night, Becky had been eavesdropping. The woman mentioned Loyalsock State Forest. It might be a coincidence, but what if it wasn't?

It wasn't likely, but if Reece somehow had Cate, she was dead. No way he'd keep her alive. He didn't torture his enemies, he eliminated them. With cold, calculated efficiency.

Samantha's eyes flew open. "Becky. You scared me."

"Found something. It might be important."

"All right. Give me a minute to use the bathroom, and I'll come into the kitchen so you can show me what you think you have." Her tone of voice betrayed her skepticism.

Well, that was fine. Maybe Becky was wrong. That would be the best-case scenario, but she couldn't sit on information that might help Malachi. Not that she cared an iota about the red-haired beauty queen, but she cared about Malachi. He was her only son and if Ezekiel wouldn't cooperate, he was her only chance of getting back into leadership in the community. If he came back to Jade, she would be important again. But she was pretty sure he wasn't going to return. From what she'd seen, he liked his life outside of her world, and she doubted she'd be able to persuade him to return. Even for his own mother. The woman who'd given him life.

Well, if the girl made him happy, then he should have her. At least she could do that much for him. But if Reece got to Cate first, her body would never be found.

Samantha met her in the kitchen as promised, and Becky explained to her what she was looking at. "We need to call the guys."

"Like you said last night. The parks and forests around here don't get great cell service. I don't know if they'll have a signal. Reece uses a booster in his camper to get one."

"Let's give it a try. If we can't reach them, I'll call my father-in-law. With his connections, we can have state police and FBI swarming the place within the hour."

The idea of so much law-enforcement made Becky's stomach lurch. Maybe it was the right thing to do. But it couldn't be, could it? Her mind traveled back to West Virginia the night when her whole world had split apart, sending everyone she loved scattering into different directions. Zeke to prison. Everyone else to various towns and states across the country. She could see it happening all over again. And it had taken so long to rebuild. Seeing it torn apart again would be too much to bear. Why couldn't they just get rid of Reece? And save the girl? Without law-enforcement interference?

Chapter Twenty-Nine

The road back toward the forest was bumpy. But this might be the only chance Cate got. She twisted in her seat to make sure Clarence wasn't watching and used her tied hands to pull the door handle. The rough texture of the cold metal felt foreign. She'd rarely been in vehicles like this one. An older model. With no shocks apparently. More potholes didn't slow her captor down. He sailed over them, jarring her teeth in her skull. She'd tried to open the door overnight to no avail, but that morning, he'd let her out of the car briefly so she could use the restroom. With any luck at all, he'd forgotten to relock her door.

Something was keeping him distracted. And his possessive comment about Becky kept replaying itself in her mind. He wasn't happy that his boss had summoned them away from his objective. But she couldn't count on the mercy of either of these men. They didn't have her best interests in mind. She had to rely on herself and God.

Lifting a prayer heavenward, she pulled the handle. The door opened and a rush of air met her as she flung herself backward out of the moving vehicle. The rear tires missed her, but not by much. Her hip made the initial impact before her head hit, leaving her stunned. A sense of urgency sliced through her head even as she reached up and felt blood pouring from her skull. It reminded her to get moving.

Rocks and debris bit into her skin. A sharp pain knifed through her shin. She ignored the agony, rose to her feet, and ran. Faster. Branches clawed her. Brakes squealed. Footsteps. Shouting. "Cate! You won't get away from me."

She hid in the base of a pine tree. Damp leaves released a musty odor. If he smelled it, she could be discovered. It was her best chance of survival. If she moved, he'd hear her, and continuing to run was out of the question. Her asthma would kill her if her captors didn't.

Clarence's footsteps. Twigs snapped under his feet. "All you'll have to show for your bravery will be cuts and bruises." He was nearby. A few trees stood between them. Her ragged breathing would give her away. She held in a cough. Her asthma brought on coughing fits. Once she started it was hard to stop. A cough now could be detrimental to her survival.

Another crunch. Leaves underfoot. He was closer. Too close. "I know you didn't get far. Come out now and I won't have to hurt you."

Seconds past. Then she heard him again. He'd passed her position. She lifted up another prayer of thanksgiving and asked that God would keep him going in the wrong direction. Then waited. Slow deep breaths. Her asthma was giving her fits, but with no inhaler, she had to practice controlled breathing, and hoped she could avoid detection. When she thought Clarence was out of earshot, she tried to figure out which way she needed to go to get to her own truck.

She'd left it off the side of the road in a pull-off. Not too far from the deer trail she'd hiked to get to the bear den. If it was close enough, it might be the best place to go. There was an inhaler in her glove box. But she had no idea how much farther it was. It could be a mile hike or it might be ten miles. They'd been headed back to the campsite where she'd been kept in the tent, but she didn't know how close they'd gotten before she took her dive.

She reached for her compass knowing it would help her to head in the right direction. It wasn't on her zipper. She'd left it in Malachi's car. Another challenge she'd need to overcome, but she could do it. Spring made some things clear. She should be able to tell direction by new growth. It was overcast, making it difficult to tell the direction of the sun at present, but they'd had strong sunshine several days over the past few weeks. If she paid close attention to the greenery and budding leaves, she'd find her way back. With the Lord's help.

She studied her surroundings and decided the best thing to do would be to follow the road, but stay far enough off it to keep from being detected. Creeping back the way she'd come, she stopped when she heard footsteps. They weren't close, but she needed to hurry. Scrambling back across the road, she scurried into the forest, but lost her footing on the slope and slid several feet before she was able to stop herself. A stream. She used the sharp edge of a stone to cut the ropes binding her wrists and then clenched and unclenched her hands as the feeling returned, leaving her with pins and needles. Making a cup from her hands, she got water. Then took several sips.

Crashing branches. Clarence closing in on her position. She'd thought she would be safe on this side of the road, but he'd found her. His taunts drew closer. "You can't hide forever." A crow squawked above as if agreeing with her tormentor. "I will find you." She hid behind a boulder the size of a small car and lifted another prayer.

BECKY SCOWLED AS SHE listened to Samantha making calls at Malachi's kitchen table. It sounded like she was coordinating an army of uniformed men and women to take down her community. Yes, she wanted Reece taken down, but not at the cost of the rest of her friends; the only family she had besides Malachi, and she barely knew him anymore. The government couldn't be trusted. They'd destroy everything. Same as they had before.

The telephone made a thud on the wooden table as Samantha set it down. "I need to run to the bathroom, so why don't you get ready to go out while I do that. We'll take Malachi's truck to the location you marked on the map. We may be able to assist them."

Becky changed back into her own clothes and then grabbed the truck keys. They were heavy in her hands. She didn't have a driver's license, but she'd driven a few times back when she was younger. Couldn't be too hard.

When she touched the cool metal of the door handle, the locks automatically opened. She looked back at the house and paused. No. This was something she needed to do. There was no turning back. The wheel was cold. Gloves would be nice. The engine didn't start at first, but when she put her foot on the brake, it roared to life. By the time she figured out how to put it into gear, Samantha flew out the front door, letting it slam behind her. Her jacket flapped in the wind as she raced toward the truck. "Wait!" Her eyes widened as she neared the truck. "You're going to need my help!"

Becky punched the button to turn on the radio and classic rock music filled the cab. She raised the volume to drown out Sam.

No. The last thing she needed was Samantha's kind of help. If she could at least rescue Clarence, she'd be all right, but without him, she'd have nothing. She never should've dismissed his offer of a life outside of Jade, but she'd clung to the hope that Ezekiel would return, or Malachi would take charge. Now everything was falling apart. And it was her own fault for telling Sam about the stupid map. That silly woman would destroy everything. She'd given it to her hoping she'd help Malachi save his girlfriend. It wasn't meant for the State Police and FBI to see. Nobody else should suffer the way she'd suffered when they took away Zeke.

Malachi was tolerating her presence, but he didn't want her there. All he cared about was his job and his redhead. No. She needed to get back to her life. Let the feds take Reece, but she had to have something to return to. A remnant of her life to hang on to. Her foot pressed down on the gas pedal and the car lurched forward.

Chapter Thirty

"Where is Clarence?" Reece slapped his hand against the table. "He should've been back here by now."

Mick smirked. "Should've let me handle it. I wouldn't have let you down."

A headache was coming on. The throbbing was a dull ache, but if left untreated it could knock him out for days. Reece rubbed his forehead. "His bucket of rust must've broken down." He tried his cell phone. Straight to voicemail. No service. That meant he was close. "Find him."

When the door slammed behind Micky, he tossed his suitcase on the bed and rifled through it until his hand circled around the pill bottle.

Soon he'd be living a new life in Philadelphia. The city that loves you back. Yeah. He'd show it some love all right. Ultimately, he planned to disappear into Texas, but it would take time to get there unnoticed. Driving straight there wasn't his wisest course of action with law-enforcement hot on his trail, so he'd spend a few weeks in Southeastern Pennsylvania before moving farther south. Maybe Alabama or Mississippi. Then over to Texas. Galveston might work. First, he needed new identification. Philadelphia. He had contacts there.

He shook two pills into his hand and filled a glass from the tap. Downed it.

Mick pushed back into the camper.

Reece scowled. "You come in without an invitation now?"

"Sorry." The kid muttered something he couldn't catch under his breath.

"What was that?"

"Nothing." Mick frowned. "I was on my way to the van when I noticed a few hikers in the woods. Thought you'd want to know."

"Are they close?"

"Near about where you grabbed the girl yesterday."

"You sure they're hikers and not cops?"

"Wasn't dressed like no cops."

Not ideal, but it'd give him a chance for some target practice. He grinned. The fog of his headache still sat heavy, which didn't bode well for his shooting accuracy, but the meds would take effect soon. In plenty of time for him to gun down the strangers be they wayward hikers or cops looking for Cate. He'd expected someone to notice she was missing sooner or later. "Forget Clarence and Cate for now. Let's give our visitors a warm welcome."

WISPS OF SMOKE ROSE from a discarded fire in the midst of the campsite. A tin can rested on its side nearby. It looked like the two RVs remaining weren't the only ones that had been there. The area was trampled with a number of flat areas where it looked like tents had recently been erected.

His guess was they hadn't been gone long. Maybe a day at most. They'd made this their personal refuge in the midst of the state forest. Vast wilderness surrounded them on every side. They must've expected to have more time before being uprooted. He wondered why they'd abandoned ship.

There was no sign of life, but the remaining campers belonged to someone. Malachi trained his binoculars on the windows of one of the campers and then the other. No movement inside. The owners wouldn't be far. But not knowing where the enemy was didn't sit well. This could be a trap.

"What if they know we're coming?" Malachi scratched his neck.

"How could they know that?" Gavin asked.

"They may have spotted us before we smelled the smoke."

Gray frowned. He could practically see the wheels turning in the big man's head. "It's a distinct possibility. Let's be smart about this. We can't all go in together. It'd make it too easy for them. When we get close, we'll split up."

"Since I have some authority as a DCNR ranger, I'll head in and confront anyone who shows their face," Malachi said.

"Give me time to get into position. I'll circle around and come at them from the back." Gavin drew a map on his left hand with his right forefinger illustrating his intentions. It made sense for him to take rearward position with his military experience, they'd be able to count on him for backup.

Before separating, they inched closer to their target. The usual forest sounds fell silent as if the wildlife expected a confrontation. His breath was steady, but his heart raced anticipating trouble. A hawk shrieked overhead reminding him they weren't the only ones hunting these woods.

Malachi patted his holster. Made eye contact with Grayson. The big man gave him a hand signal to let him know he would approach from the right. Malachi would take the most direct route and confront them head on. If there was anyone around. Gavin moved out. Malachi lifted a prayer that they wouldn't get themselves killed trying to save Cate. Then another prayer for her safety.

AS BECKY WOUND HER way down the narrow logging road, the truck scraped against tree branches. She was driving too fast, but she needed to sit forward on the seat to reach the pedal and that didn't leave her much control. There was no little handle under the seat to adjust it manually. There had to be a way, but she was in too much of a hurry to take the time to figure it out.

The ruts in the road jolted her teeth and spine, but she kept going. If she could get there first, she could warn the others before the FBI arrived.

It wasn't far. She had to be getting close, but she couldn't tell. Her sense of direction never was the best. Then she saw it. The outline of a camper. She tapped the button to stop the truck's engine, but it wouldn't stop. No matter. She opened the door and climbed out. The F150 rolled forward. Uh-oh. Something wasn't right. She jumped out of the way. The sound of twisting metal reverberated through the forest before silence reigned. Even the birds ceased their chatter. The crash would give her position away, but that was the least of her worries.

At least she had Malachi's gun. She'd end Reece's life the same way he'd ended Byron's. The man he claimed as a brother. Bile rose in her throat as she was transported back to their execution. The smell of blood mingled with the loamy woodsy scents. The screams for mercy. The quiet of the forest following the sharp report of the gunshots. It was a nightmare she couldn't stop reliving. And it was Reece's fault. Yes, she'd told Reece what they'd said, so she bore some blame. He'd killed them. She hadn't done that. But she had remained silent knowing they would die.

After one last glance at the damage to the front of Malachi's truck, she removed the weapon from her waistband and stalked toward the camper. Twigs snapped underfoot as she approached. The spot where she'd spent the past week was gone. Someone had taken down her tent. A few more steps allowed her to see the area better. Nobody was near the campfire. And that's when she noticed it. All the tents were gone. It was eerily quiet. Only two campers remained on the site. Everyone else was gone. They'd left her behind. A physical pain in her chest, sharp and heavy all at once, brought her to her knees. Stones bit into her bare knees and tears stung her eyes, but she welcomed the pain. Falling forward, she gave in to emotion welling up inside her. Her body wracked with sobs. Once they started, she couldn't stop them. Nothing would ever be as it once was.

Chapter Thirty-One

The sky remained overcast, making it difficult to pinpoint the position of the sun, but she'd been walking for hours. Midmorning best Cate could tell. She rounded a corner and spotted something blue in the distance. Looked like a parked vehicle. Her work truck was white. Was someone else out here looking for her? Another cult member?

She stepped back into the forest and inhaled the damp earth mixed with pine. It smelled like snow. If they were going to get another storm, she ought to find shelter. Fast. Following the tree line, she moved closer until she could check out what she'd seen. She needed to get a better look before the driver saw her. When she parted the branches of a spruce and peered out, something skittered near her feet. A robin. The worms must be abundant after the snow melt. A smile touched her lips despite her own troubles.

Refocusing on her quarry, she sucked in a sharp breath. A blue Bronco. Not many of them around. Pushing out a relieved breath, she smiled. Grayson. He'd come looking for her. He wasn't in there. Which meant he was in the woods somewhere. Hopefully, not confronting her kidnappers. She wasn't sure whom she should worry about, the cult members who had abducted her, or her brother.

She ran across the road and entered the code for the keyless entry all while praying he hadn't changed it. It unlocked and she let herself in and immediately pushed the console back and opened the safe beneath it where Gray always kept a spare nine-millimeter handgun. It was a Sig Sauer. Same as the one he'd purchased for her. She released the magazine and checked the chamber. Gratitude filled her that it was fully loaded.

Leaning back in the seat, she took a few deep breaths. Before long, she'd need to look for her brother. It wasn't safe out there with a killer on the loose. Grayson wouldn't know Reece's plans to use her to get to Malachi and his biological mother. Or how he planned to take them both out. Without all the facts, he was out there unprepared. Maybe she could get somewhere safe and call for help. That might be the smartest move, but there might not be time. They'd taken her cell, so by the time she reached somewhere from which to make the call, it might be too late. Going back into the woods was the only real answer.

He'd flip out if he knew she was contemplating following him. But he'd come all this way to rescue her. Her brothers and their wives had been there for her when the Continental Alliance had taken her captive. The least she could do was return the favor.

A quick search for supplies was in order. A blanket in the back might come in handy, and the fold-up tote bag stuffed in the back of the seat would make a decent backpack if she laced some rope through it. Too bad she'd disposed of the ropes they'd used to bind her hands. She checked the glove compartment, hoping to find something to snack on. An MRE didn't look all that appetizing, but beneath it she discovered a couple of granola bars. Jenna must've hidden them there. Her health nut brother certainly didn't. Something flashy caught her eye. It was a key fob. The car didn't require a key. With the fob, she could start it. Taking note of her surroundings to make sure she could return to the same spot, she put her foot on the brake and started the engine. Her brother didn't leave his keys behind. Ever. It had to be divine intervention. She lifted a prayer. *Thank you, Jesus.* Sweet warmth filled the space as she pulled out. Her truck couldn't be far and before she attempted any more hiking, she needed to get her inhaler.

Becky wiped her sleeve across her face to dry her tears and drew in a shaky breath as she pulled herself up. A pine cone crunched underfoot as she moved to recline against a birch tree. The forest was dense here. Not many leaves yet, but tiny buds adorned most trees, and she knew that just beyond here was a large clearing. But she needed to get back to her son's truck and drive herself out of here. If she hadn't killed the engine.

Crash.

She looked around but couldn't find the source. She hoped she hadn't caused a tree to fall with her poor parking skills. A bird sang, drawing Becky out of her wallowing. She surveyed her surroundings for the splash of color that would indicate the type of bird she'd heard, but instead of finding one, her gaze lit upon a man crouched behind a boulder. Her pulse quickened. It was Gavin. Samantha's husband. The one who'd left Malachi's house last night to come help him find Cate. She wanted to run over and ask him where Malachi was, but something kept her rooted in place. What if something had happened to her son?

Gavin made the call again then panicked eyes met hers and she realized he hadn't known she was there. He gestured for her to stay put before pointing at something behind Reece's camper. Her eyes widened and her posture straightened as she saw Reece walk up behind Grayson Garrison.

MALACHI WALKED INTO THE center of the camping area and approached the fire ring before drawing his Glock and holding it down at his side. Finger safely off the trigger, but safety off and ready to fire should the need arise. He used his left hand to rap on the camper door. No response. He moved to the other RV. Still nothing but silence. He did a visual sweep of the area before peering in the windows of one of the campers. A suitcase lay open atop the bed. Inside, he could see shaving lotion and men's deodorant. Other than the luggage, everything was cleaned up. Nothing remained behind.

At least one straggler was around here somewhere, and they weren't leaving without talking to him.

The roar of a vehicle. It was out of sight. He couldn't find the source. A crashing noise. Possibly from the car. Then all was calm. Too calm. A bluebird perched at the edge of the clearing. It dived, retrieved a meal, and resituated itself on a nearby log.

A loud bang came from nearby. A tree falling? Maybe just a branch. A cardinal called. Something was off. His spine stiffened. On high alert, he raised his weapon but froze, his breath caught in his throat when his gaze took in Grayson's prone form. Unconscious.

Maurice Moretti aimed his weapon straight at Gray's head. "Seems we're in a standoff, Mr. James."

"Guess so." Malachi steadied his weapon, keeping it directed at center mass.

Chapter Thirty-Two

Cate pulled up behind her truck, ready to grab her medicine. A sigh escaped when she patted her pocket only to find it empty. Her mind flashed back to the moment on the log when she'd been watching their campsite through her binoculars and Reece had approached from behind. The steel had been cold against her head. When he'd grabbed her from the trail, he'd taken her backpack. Her keys were in it along with everything else she'd brought.

But she couldn't dwell on that now. If her brother was with Reece, his life might be in danger. She needed to find out, but she couldn't head in there unprepared. Her breathing wasn't as ragged as it had been earlier after her run through the forest, but another attack could happen at any time. She needed that inhaler. The idea of breaking a window on her work vehicle didn't sit well, but it might be her only choice.

An idea hit her. She climbed into the bed of the truck and pushed at the rear sliding glass. The thing never operated smoothly, but it didn't lock right either. The glass budged. Just barely. She slid her hand in the narrow space she'd created and strained as she pressed her palm against the edge of the stubborn window, trying to force it open. A breath escaped as it gave way. Her sore ribs rubbed against the sides as she squeezed through the tiny space. She pushed through the pain, wincing as her hips went through and she toppled head first onto the seat.

Once inside, she righted herself, straightened her shirt, and searched her glove box for her inhaler. She found two of them stuffed inside. She inhaled, letting the medication fill her lungs, and held her breath to give it time to do its work. Stuffing it into her pocket, she exhaled and her chest expanded as she took another deep breath and let herself out of the truck. A second draw on her inhaler would have to wait until she was behind the wheel. Time wasn't on her side, so she needed to get going. Her brother's life might depend on it.

Branches swayed and the leaves that littered the side of the road rustled when the wind picked up as if hurrying her along as she hoofed it back to her brother's Bronco. His vehicle would fare far better on the logging road than her work truck would. It was made for off-roading. And this definitely qualified.

Malachi's jaw hardened as he kept his weapon pointed at Reece Mclean. He forced his teeth to unclench and relaxed his stance. If he needed to shoot, tense muscles could cause him to miss his target. Relax and squeeze. His instructor's simple commands replayed in his mind.

"Drop your weapon, or I'll put a bullet hole in your buddy here." Reece smiled. The creep seemed to be enjoying the standoff.

Lord, now would be a great time to intervene. "What's keeping you from shooting us both once I drop my weapon?"

Reece chuckled. "You have something or rather someone I want."

"And whom would that be?"

"Rebecca Groves. I think your life for hers is a fair trade. I'd send you to get her, but something tells me you'd call all your law-enforcement buddies. So, since my man has your little girlfriend, I'll send her to get your mother and bring her back. I don't think she'd do anything so dumb as call in reinforcements."

Malachi's jaw clenched, and he tightened his grip on his weapon. "Leave Cate alone."

"Sorry, no can do."

Something moved on the periphery of Malachi's vision as he held his gun hand steady. Another cardinal call. No. It wasn't a bird at all. Gavin was to the east of the gunman. Might've been nice to know ahead of time that he'd planned to communicate with bird calls.

"What do you want with Becky, anyway?" Malachi swallowed hard as he tried to keep Reece focused on him, so he wouldn't notice Gavin's approach.

Malachi stepped back but kept his weapon trained on Reece as he waited to see what Gavin had planned.

"Set the gun down, Mr. James." Reece's voice was calm and smooth. Like someone discussing contracts in a boardroom. "I may be persuaded to let you live if you cooperate."

"Place yours on the ground first." Malachi focused on Reece's face. The last thing he wanted on his conscience was Grayson's death. And allowing Reece to gain the upper hand would guarantee disaster. As long as they both had weapons, Malachi retained some control. Reece wouldn't shoot Gray as long as he knew he'd be killed the moment he did.

Malachi's pulse raced when a flash of ginger hair appeared just behind and to the west of Reece's location. His eyes widened, his mouth dropped open, and his spine stiffened. Why would she put herself in danger if she'd escaped? If he could grab her and shake her without lowering his weapon, he would. But right now, he had to trust that Gavin had a plan. Some way to put an end to this standoff. He watched Gavin through his periphery, afraid if he glanced that way, he'd give away his position.

"I'm here!" Cate's voice gave away her location, ending any hope Malachi had of her presence going unnoticed. "I don't know what happened to Clarence. I jumped out of his truck while he was driving."

"And you came back here?" Reece laughed and raised an eyebrow at Malachi. "Not the brightest bulb, is she?"

Malachi's nostrils flared, and he tightened his grip on the pistol.

"Well, be a good girl and come out in front so I can see you without turning my head." Reece winked.

Malachi's blood turned to lava. He could strangle him with his bare hands and think nothing of it in that moment. Lifting a prayer, he took another deep breath and forced his hand to remain steady.

"I'll surrender, but I won't help you get Becky. I'm not willing to endanger anyone else." Cate raised her trembling hands above her head and moved forward, positioning herself between Reece and Grayson. She planned to protect her brother with her own body. Her bravery was incredible. And aggravating. A shift in the wind brought a dark cloud in to cover what little sun they'd had. A storm was moving in.

"Well, love, you're not the one I want, so while it's noble of you to surrender yourself, if you aren't going to get Becky, I might as well kill the lot of you. You're no good to me."

The first fat rain drop fell on Malachi's nose as someone crashed through the trees near where Gavin was positioned. "I'm the one you want. And I'm right here! Don't hurt anyone else." Becky dropped to her knees facing Reece. She held a gun of her own, but her gun hand was raised in the air as she positioned herself between them. This couldn't be happening. His girlfriend and his biological mother both trying to give up their lives to save him and the Garrison men. That kind of sacrificial love was rare. Not something he'd felt often in his life, but he'd sensed it from his Lord and Savior. He tried to stay focused enough to keep his gun hand steady as the weight of it grew heavier the longer the standoff continued. He drew in a measured breath and lifted another prayer as the muzzle of Reece's handgun changed targets from Cate to Becky. The sky opened up in a downpour, lowering visibility and magnifying the threat. Even if they made it out of this alive, they needed to make their way down the mountain along a twisty logging road that wasn't suitable for quads let alone vehicles.

A sudden shift in Reece's demeanor warned Malachi that it was now or never. He lifted a prayer even as he squeezed off a round. Then another. His hands shook as he lowered his weapon. Simultaneously, two men joined the melee. One man he didn't recognize tackled Reece to the ground and subdued him while Gavin cuffed him. But Malachi stood frozen in place, letting the rain water wash over him. He'd never shot a man before. The shot had been textbook center mass as he'd been trained and had drilled into him in practice. Nothing had prepared him for the reality though. He may have taken a human life.

Chapter Thirty-Three

Becky's heart leapt into her throat as she awaited the gunshot that would end her life. The crack of a weapon filled the air. Nothing happened. She wasn't hit. Another shot. Her pulse raced as Clarence crashed through the underbrush and jumped on top of Reece. A flash of blood. Malachi took a step forward. Understanding dawned. Malachi had taken the shot. Gavin joined Clarence and grabbed Reece's hands, twisting them behind his back, pinning them in place, then wrapping zip ties around them.

It all happened faster than the space of two breaths, but she felt like she watched it all happen in slow motion.

Reece was hit. She wasn't. Clarence appeared at her side and helped her to rise to her feet before crushing her to his chest.

He was here. Hadn't left with the others. "Don't ever do that again, woman, or I'll shoot you myself." She smiled at the strain evident in his voice. He truly cared about her. Maybe Clarence was her future. It was time to let go of the memories of her life with Zeke. Look to something new with the man who'd been right there beside her all along.

"SOMEONE SHOULD PROBABLY CALL 911." Malachi's voice shook with the strain of having taken the shot that might've ended another man's life.

"I already hear sirens, but it couldn't hurt to direct them this way." Gavin grabbed some gauze from his backpack and stuffed it into Reece's wound.

"I'll call." The man who helped Gavin tackle Reece rose to his feet and walked closer to the camper before dialing.

Malachi returned his attention to Gavin. "Is he alive?"

"For now. Can't promise he'll stay that way though." Gavin frowned at Cate. "What were you thinking? You could've been killed."

Tears spilled down Cate's cheeks. "And what about you?" Her voice was just above a whisper. "I could've lost all three of you within minutes of each other. Why would you put yourself in that kind of danger?"

Malachi drew her into his arms. "I think I speak for all three of us when I say we would do anything to protect you."

"Right back at you." She buried her head in his chest.

CATE ROSE TO HER tiptoes and gave Malachi a lingering kiss in the rain. She'd always wanted to kiss a man in the rain. She dismissed the thought and refocused on her surroundings. "You should see to your mother."

As he walked to where his mother talked with the man who'd tackled Reece. Wait. It was Clarence. Why had he tackled his boss? Clarence's eyes softened as he looked down at Becky. The creep was in love with Malachi's mother. No doubt about it. Was that why he'd been so determined to find her? Could he have been planning on protecting her all along? If so, his motives for keeping Cate captive may have been less sinister than she'd initially believed. But still despicable. If he'd asked for her help to protect Becky, she would've done so without having to fling herself from a moving vehicle. Even as the thought crossed her mind, she felt the scrapes and bruises from the ordeal. It'd been a long day and if she had to guess, she'd say it was barely noon.

Gavin knelt beside Grayson's prone figure and he slapped him, trying to wake him up. Cate got down beside them and checked Gray's pulse. It was strong and steady. She pinched him, and his eyes fluttered open.

"Two can play at that game." His voice had a groggy quality as if he'd just awakened from anesthesia.

"You okay?"

"Depends."

"On what?"

"Where am I? And who are you?"

Her eyes widened, and she studied his face. Her breathing was ragged. She might need her inhaler again. Gray didn't recognize her. Her eldest brother had amnesia. No. She closed her eyes for a moment. This wasn't okay.

Then he let out a full belly laugh. "Had you going there, didn't I?"

Gavin rolled his eyes.

She smacked him lightly and shook her head. "You think you're so funny, but I'm telling Jenna you scared the wits out of me."

Gray smirked as he sat up, wiped the mud from his hands, and glanced around. "Just trying to lighten things up."

"I should probably tell you... I borrowed the Bronco."

"You did what!?"

"Needed to get up here in a hurry to save your skin."

He shook his head. "Seems like I missed most of the action."

"Count your blessings." Gavin swiped his sleeve over his forehead. "Our buddy over there threatened to blow your brains out before turning his pistol on our baby sister." He faced her. "What were you thinking? You should've stayed out of it and let us handle it."

"He was about to kill Gray. I couldn't just hide in the woods."

Turning back to Gray, he pointed to his head. "Be glad he knocked you out. Best you weren't awake to see how serious the situation was. I was about two seconds away from taking a risky shot when Malachi took out the threat without hesitation."

The rain let up and only a light drizzle remained. Sirens grew louder and chopper blades whirred overhead. She stared up at the sky. "I guess they're going to take Reece to the hospital."

Gavin glanced at Reece's figure lying flat in the mud only feet away from where they stood. He folded an arm around her shoulder and gave her a squeeze. "No worries. If Moretti survives, he'll be kept guarded until he's moved to a secure facility.

They don't let wanted men freely wander around hospitals."

"Thanks for coming to my rescue. I should've known all three of you would be here, not just Gray."

He smiled. "Have we ever let you down?"

Chapter Thirty-Four

The loamy scent of wet forest earth rose up to greet him as Malachi jogged to Kevin's truck. His friend opened the door, but they waited to speak until the wind died down and the sounds of the chopper faded as it lifted away with Moretti on board.

"From what I heard over the radio, it looks like you got yourself into quite a mess."

"No doubt about it." Malachi shook the other man's hand. "Look, I know I don't always play well with others."

Kevin crossed his arms over his chest. "You won't get an argument from me."

"I'm trying to apologize for being an idiot and not telling you everything from the start. About my biological parents."

"Well, stop trying and just say you're sorry already." Kevin's grin proved he was enjoying the moment of humility a little too much for Malachi's comfort.

"Sorry." Malachi picked up a leaf and twirled it between his thumb and forefinger.

"Water under the bridge. You ready to get out of here? Doesn't look like your personal vehicle fared too well."

"Wait. What are you talking about?"

Kevin gestured down the logging road. "Hit a tree about a quarter of a mile down."

"How did it even get here?" He scratched his chin.

Becky cleared her throat behind him, so he faced her. She avoided eye contact as she spoke in a mousy voice. "I kind of stole it."

"You what?" He couldn't keep the tension out of his voice. Letting the woman stay in his house had been a mistake. He'd known it from the start.

"I needed to warn the other members of Jade that Samantha called the authorities. I thought about what happened back in West Virginia when your father was arrested. It looked like history was going to repeat itself."

"That situation was completely different. This time they were only after Reece. He was the only person they were after."

She frowned, and her jaw took on a hard set to it. "It was a chance I couldn't take."

Kevin patted his shoulder, grounding him in the moment. Getting worked up over a truck after the morning they'd just had was beyond ridiculous. He lifted a prayer for serenity, and shook his head before rubbing his forehead and exhaling.

"Don't worry about the truck. It's insured." His remaining agitation was apparent from his tone, but that couldn't be helped. He turned back to Kevin. "Can you get Becky to wherever the troopers are doing their interviews? I want to check on Cate before I leave here. And I'll have to see if my truck is drivable."

"Yeah. Sure thing." Kevin saluted and led Malachi's mother away. As annoying as the truck thing was, Rebecca's behavior that morning had been motherly. She'd literally put herself in front of a loaded gun. That willingness to sacrifice her own life for his demonstrated her love for him, despite their tumultuous past. His foster parents would always be his family, but maybe he could find room in his life for Becky, too. He wouldn't be calling her 'mom' anytime soon, but he didn't need to shut her out completely.

As he headed back toward the fray, his eyes locked with Cate's, and she gave him a slow smile.

Cate's stomach fluttered as Malachi's gaze locked on her and his steps brought him closer. Her own feet moved of their own volition, meeting him in the middle. Catching her in a crushing hug, he tucked her close to him, and she buried her face in his neck. "I can't breathe."

"Sorry." He loosened his grip. "Please never put me through that again. If you had been shot—I don't even want to think about it."

"I wasn't, so let's not go there." She wrapped her arms around his neck and played with the curled edges of his damp hair. It was smooth and soft under her fingertips. She kissed his neck and trailed more kisses across the rough texture of his bearded chin until she reached his lips.

He kissed her back with an abandon she hadn't known he possessed. She was certain he'd forgotten where they were by the ragged edge to his breath as it mingled with hers. That is until her brother cleared his throat behind them. Malachi locked eyes with her and then closed his. She followed his example and prepared for the teasing she knew her brothers would heap upon them. They turned to face them, and Malachi hooked his arm around her shoulder.

Grayson grinned. "The state police agreed to do interviews at the park office so we wouldn't have to drive all the way to the barracks. You ready to go?"

"She's coming with me. Just give me one second to make sure my truck still drives." He released her and trudged down the path that would lead to his truck.

When he was out of earshot, Gray raised an eyebrow. "You letting a man speak for you now?"

"Nah. But I am going with him. We have some unfinished business to take care of."

"Kissy face stuff." Gavin joined the conversation and made obnoxious smooching sounds.

"You two are too much. Maybe that's why I want to ride with Malachi. To get away from you." She wanted to know what happened next. His kiss seemed to indicate that he was serious about her, but she needed words. Reassurance.

Gray winked. "I think you two are a good match. He'll do right by you."

"You're giving him the Grayson Garrison stamp of approval?" She tapped her foot. "There must be something wrong with him. I thought he was okay, but if you like him..."

Malachi returned and gave her brothers a nod. "Looks like it's running, but if you wouldn't mind following us in case it stalls out, that'd be great."

"That oughta keep you two from pulling over for a make-out session." Gavin chuckled at his own joke.

Malachi rolled his eyes then laced his fingers through hers. "Your brothers are something else."

She smiled. "Yes. They certainly are. But I wouldn't trade them for the world."

Chapter Thirty-Five

Sunlight flooded through the windshield, warming the interior. A welcome change after the overcast and rainy morning. He was just glad the snow never materialized. The drive back to the park office didn't take nearly enough time. He needed time with Cate. Preferably a lifetime, but that was something he wasn't quite ready to share with her yet. However, they did need to talk about the future and their roles in each other's lives. It was too soon to talk about marriage. Even though the idea kept beating him over the head like a baseball bat. But Cate deserved a proper courtship, and he would give her one.

He reached for her left hand as she was pulling the door handle with her right. "You mind hanging out in the truck for a few more minutes?"

Her smile was answer enough. "I'd stay here with you all day, but you know we'll only have a few minutes before my brothers start knocking on the windows."

"I don't doubt that." He groaned. "Your brothers aren't going to leave you here. We may not get any more time alone today."

She frowned. "Those creeps stole the keys to my work truck along with everything else in my backpack, including my identification, so I will need to get a ride from them. I'm going to have a few days of fun ahead of me getting all that sorted out. I also have to check on Penny. I'm sure my landlady noticed my absence and took care of her, but I need that assurance."

"Yeah. I left Becky with Titan and Pixie, but I think Gavin's wife is still at my house, so I'm sure she took care of them when my mother split."

"I'm certain you're right. She's a park ranger, you know? Just like you. Definite animal lover. And excellent sister-in-law."

Malachi chuckled. "Good to know." He threaded his fingers with hers.

The air thickened between them, and the desire to tell her how he felt about her burned strong. "So?"

Silence hung between them until she squeezed his hand. "You're asking what now?"

"Exactly. Where do we go from here?"

"I'm all in if you are."

"I am." She stared at their joined hands, and he lifted them to his lips and kissed the back of her hand. "I can work from anywhere in the state. Maybe I can get a place near here for now," she said.

He nodded. "Or I could transfer to a state park closer to you."

A smile tipped her lips up. "You would do that?"

"I'll do whatever it takes, Cate. I love you."

"You do?"

He cupped her chin and kissed her gently. "I do."

"I love you, too." She slid closer on the seat and rested her head against his shoulder.

His heart felt full. The woman he'd fallen for reciprocated his feelings. Everything he ever wanted was within his grasp. God was good. All the time. And He would work out their future in whatever way brought Him the most glory. Malachi bent down and kissed the top of her head where the sun warmed the golden red strands.

The prophesied knocking came in the form of Gavin rapping his knuckles against the windshield and waving a hand for them to hurry up. She closed her eyes briefly before opening them again and giving him a resigned smile. "So much for alone time. I have to work out the details with Virginia, but we're going to place that last bear cub in Loyalsock near where that monster grabbed me."

"You want me to come along again?"

"I'd like that."

"So would I." He kissed her one last time before exiting the truck and opening the passenger door for her.

* * *

Epilogue

Cate found a seat and soaked in the activity. There was something about early autumn that brought out the best in everyone present. A few of Malachi's siblings kicked around a soccer ball while his foster parents sat on matching Adirondack chairs nearby.

They hadn't heard from Becky since Reece's hospitalization and subsequent arrest. Malachi hadn't said much about her absence, but she sensed it nagged at him.

Since they were at Gavin and Samantha's house, Cate's brothers and their wives played host to their guests. Cate's dad had business in Paris, so he couldn't attend. Understandable. Who cancels a meeting for a picnic? Even so, she wished he was there. It'd been a while since she'd seen him and she missed him. Watching Malachi's dad interact with everyone made her own father's absence all the more noticeable, but she tucked the feeling away to deal with later.

When Malachi's youngest sister, Keisha, took the seat across from her, Cate rested her elbows on the picnic table and listened intently as she regaled her with a story about the guy she'd met at her new job working at the library.

"Do you like this boy?" Cate asked.

"No. Why would you think that?" Keisha squished up her face. "I told you how annoying he is. He comes in every afternoon with a different book question. What's up with that? He's weird."

"Maybe he's just looking for an excuse to talk to you?"

"Whatever." She rose from her seat. "He can find someone else to bother. I'm going to grab a burger. Want one?"

Cate stood. "Sure. I'll join you."

Gavin flipped a burger onto a bun for each of them and bowed at the waist like he'd just performed a magic trick. She laughed at his antics and met Keisha's smiling eyes. "If you think your brothers are weird, wait until you get to know mine."

"I'm pretty sure Malachi is weirder than your brothers."

"Not so," Cate said.

"I'll bet your brothers don't play with bear cubs."

"No. They don't, but they protect rich celebrities. I think that's worse."

"It is not."

"Well, maybe I don't think Malachi's weird because I like bears, too. Who do you think your brother was with when he placed those cubs?"

"Really? You work with wild animals?"

"I do." She grinned. "I'm a wildlife biologist. It's the best job in the world." At least it was when there weren't crazed assassins lurking about.

"Maybe I should do that."

"I thought you wanted to be a librarian?"

"I don't know what I want."

"That's okay. Just enjoy these years. You can decide when you're ready."

"Mom says I should pray about it. It's best to ask for God's will before you commit to a career path."

"Your mother is a wise woman."

Malachi approached from behind and put an arm around each of them and squeezed. "How are my two favorite girls?"

"Better now that you're here." Cate smiled up at him.

"Gross. I'm going to go find Jared." Keisha set her plate down, picked up her burger, and skipped off toward the group playing soccer.

Malachi took Cate's plate from her hand and carried it over to the table. He sat beside her and waited until she took a giant bite of the juicy burger before speaking. "I know we haven't been together long, but I was thinking maybe, that you might, possibly want to consider..."

She swallowed. "Spit it out already."

"Marry me, Cate?" He held out a diamond ring.

She raised a brow. "I expected a jade ring."

"Not funny. Will you marry me or not?"

"I will." Applause broke out all around them. "Everyone here knew you were going to propose?"

"Yep." Malachi lifted her from her seat, pulled her into his arms, and kissed her thoroughly. She could see them together in twenty-five years seated side by side like Malachi's parents watching their own family grow. Her arms tightened around him, and she rested her head on his chest.

If you haven't read the first two books in this series: Grave Pursuits and Grave Secrets, you can grab them from my website at https://ElleEKay.com or from your favorite retailer.

ALSO BY ELLE E. KAY

Endless Mountain Series

Shadowing Stella

Implicating Claudia

Chasing Sofie

The Lawkeepers Contemporary Romance Series

Lawfully Held

A K-9 Lawkeeper Romance

Lawfully Defended

A SWAT Lawkeeper Romance

Lawfully Guarded

A Billionaire Bodyguard Lawkeeper Romance

The Lawkeepers Historical Romance Series

Lawfully Taken

A Bounty Hunter Lawkeeper Romance

Lawfully Given

A Christmas Lawkeeper Romance

Lawfully Promised

A Texas Ranger Lawkeeper Romance

Lawfully Vindicated

A US Marshal Lawkeeper Romance

Blushing Brides Series

The Billionaire's Reluctant Bride

The Bodyguard's Fake Bride

Heroes of Freedom Ridge Series

Healing the Hero

A Christian Army Ranger Christmas Romance

Persuaded by the Hero
A CHRISTIAN ARMY VETERAN CHRISTMAS ROMANCE
Inspired by the Hero
A CHRISTIAN PHYSICIAN ASSISTANT CHRISTMAS ROMANCE

Christmas in Redemption Ridge Series
Wooing the Widower

Pennsylvania Parks Series
Grave Pursuits
Grave Secrets
Grave Consequences

Standalone Novella
Holly's Noel

ABOUT AUTHOR

Elle E. Kay lives in Central Pennsylvania. She loves life in the country on her hobby farm with her husband, Joe. Elle is a born-again Christian with a deep faith and love for the Lord Jesus Christ. She desires to live for Him and to put Him first in everything she does.

You can connect with Elle on her website and blog at https://www.elleekay.com/ or on social media:

Facebook: www.facebook.com/ElleEKay7

Instagram: www.instagram.com/elleekay7

ACKNOWLEDGEMENTS

I WOULD LIKE TO give special thanks to my husband, Joe Kelleher, who is a constant source of encouragement.

A special thanks also goes out to my editor, Patti Geesey, who does a remarkable job of helping me polish my work. A shoutout also goes to my beta readers who make sure to catch any errors before publication. Also, a big thanks go to my ARC readers and street team for reviewing my books and sharing about them.

I'd also like to extend my thanks to you, my readers. It is my prayer that my books touch hearts and draw souls closer to the Lord Jesus Christ. I'd also like to extend my gratitude to you, my readers. Without your support, I wouldn't be able to do what I do. It is my prayer that my books touch hearts and draw souls closer to the Lord Jesus Christ.

This story is a product of my imagination and a work of

fiction. Names, characters, businesses, places, events, locales, and incidents are either the products of my imagination or in the case of actual towns, historical persons, and companies mentioned, they have been used in a fictitious manner. Any resemblance to actual persons, living or dead, or actual events is purely coincidental.

Any errors or deficiencies are my own.

Personal Testimony

I first came to know Jesus as a young teen, but before long I strayed from God and allowed my selfish desires to rule me. I sought after acceptance and love from my peers, not knowing that only God could fill my emptiness. My teen years were full of angst and misery, for me and my family. People I loved were hurt by my selfishness. My heartache was at times overwhelming, but I couldn't find the healing I desperately desired. After several runaway attempts my family was left with little choice, and they put me in a group home/residential facility where I would get the constant supervision I needed.

At that home I met a godly man called 'Big John' who tried once again to draw me back to Jesus. He would point out Matthew 11:28-30 and remind me that all I had to do to find peace was give my cares to Christ. I wanted to live a Christian life, but something kept pulling me away. The cycle continued well into adulthood. I would call out to God, but then I would turn away from Him. (If you read the Old Testament, you'll see that the nation of Israel had a similar pattern, they would call out to God and He would heal them and bring them back into their land. Then they would stray, and He would chastise them. It was a cycle that went on and on).

When I came to realize that God's love was still available to me despite all my failings, I found peace and joy that have remained with me to this day. It wasn't God who kept walking away. He'd placed his seal on me in childhood and no matter how far I ran from Him, **He remained faithful.** When I finally recognized His unfailing love, I was made free.

2 Timothy 2:13

"If we believe not, yet he abideth faithful: he cannot deny himself."

Ephesians 4:30

"And grieve not the holy Spirit of God, whereby ye are sealed unto the day of redemption."

I let myself be drawn into His loving arms and led by His precious nail-scarred hands. He has kept me securely at His side and taught me important life lessons. Jesus has given me back the freedom I had in Christ on that day when I accepted the precious gift He'd offered. My life in Him is so much fuller than it ever was when I tried to live by the world's standards.

I implore you, if you've known Jesus and strayed, call out to Him.

If you've never known Jesus Christ as your personal Lord and Saviour. Find out what it means to have a relationship with Christ. Not religion, but a personal relationship with a loving God.

God makes it clear in His word that there isn't a person

righteous enough to get to heaven on their own.

Romans 3:10

"As it is written, There is none righteous, no, not one:"

We are all sinners.

Romans 3:23

"For all have sinned, and come short of the glory of God;"

Death is the penalty for sin.

Romans 6:23

"For the wages of sin is death; but the gift of God is eternal life through Jesus Christ our Lord."

Christ died on the cross for our sins.

Romans 5:8

"But God commendeth his love toward us, in that, while we were yet sinners, Christ died for us."

If we confess and believe we will be saved.

Romans 10:9

"That if thou shalt confess with thy mouth the Lord Jesus, and shalt believe in thine heart that God hath raised him from the dead, thou shalt be saved."

Once we believe He sets us free.

Romans 8:1

"There is therefore now no condemnation to them which are in Christ Jesus, who walk not after the flesh, but after the Spirit."

I hope you'll take hold of that freedom and start a personal relationship with Christ Jesus.

Made in the USA
Middletown, DE
15 May 2024